PENGUI

WHERE THEY

Lucy Caldwell was born in Belfast in 1981. In 2005 she won the PMA Award for Most Promising Playwright, and was on attachment to the National Theatre Studio. Her first full-length play, *Leaves*, won the 2006 George Devine Award. *Where They Were Missed* was longlisted for the inaugural Dylan Thomas Prize. Lucy Caldwell is currently under commission to write for the main stage at London's Royal Court Theatre. She lives in East London.

Where They Were Missed

LUCY CALDWELL

PENGUIN BOOKS

For my parents and for my sisters and for our childhood

PENGUIN BOOKS

Published by the Penguin Group

Penguin Books Ltd, 80 Strand, London WC2R ORL, England

Penguin Group (USA) Inc., 375 Hudson Street, New York, New York 10014, USA

Penguin Group (Canada), 90 Eglinton Avenue East, Suite 700, Toronto, Ontario, Canada M4P 2Y3
(a division of Pearson Penguin Canada Inc.)

Penguin Ireland, 25 St Stephen's Green, Dublin 2, Ireland (a division of Penguin Books Ltd)

Penguin Group (Australia), 250 Camberwell Road, Camberwell, Victoria 3124, Australia
(a division of Pearson Australia Group Pty Ltd)

Penguin Books India Pvt Ltd, 11 Community Centre, Panchsheel Park, New Delhi – 110 017, India

Penguin Group (NZ), 67 Apollo Drive, Rosedale, North Shore 0632, New Zealand
(a division of Pearson New Zealand Ltd)

Penguin Books (South Africa) (Pty) Ltd, 24 Sturdee Avenue, Rosebank, Johannesburg 2196, South Africa

Penguin Books Ltd, Registered Offices: 80 Strand, London WC2R ORL, England

www.penguin.com

First published by Viking 2006
Published in Penguin Books 2007

1

Grateful acknowledgement is made for permission to reproduce extracts from the following:
Early Irish Myths and Sagas, translated with an introduction by Jeffrey Gantz (Penguin Classics, 1981).
'Selva Oscura', by Louis MacNeice, *Selected Poems* (Faber & Faber, 1988)

Set in Monotype Dante
by Palimpsest Book Production Limited, Grangemouth, Stirlingshire
Printed in England by Clays Ltd, St Ives plc

ISBN: 978-0-141-02429-5

A house can be haunted by those who were never there
If there was where they were missed. Returning to such
Is it worse if you miss the same or another or none?
The haunting anyway is too much.
You have to leave the house to clear the air.

Louis MacNeice, 'Selva Oscura'

Thanks to Peter Straus; Rowan Routh; Mary Mount.

To Maura Dooley; Stephen Knight; Blake Morrison; Ian Patterson; Alice Carey.

And to the other friends who read and reread and helped and encouraged; you know who you are.

PART ONE
Belfast

I

Belfast is hot. Belfast is never hot. But Belfast is hot this summer. Daddy says it's the hottest summer in Living Memory. Mammy says, It's hot as hell. The air is sweaty, and it hangs in sheets; sucking the breath out of you, Mammy says, and it makes my and Daisy's damp ponytails itch the backs of our necks. The Orangemen are marching at the bottom of our street, singing songs of men who died long ago. Their music makes you want to stand tall and stamp your feet in time to the drums, but Mammy keeps the windows of our house shut tight; if me or Daisy or Daddy leave a window open by accident, and Mammy hears that music, she spits on the floor, a long thin string of yellow, and she slams the window so hard the glass shivers. The Orange music gives Mammy such a sore head that some days she doesn't get up out of bed at all. The other children on our street go with their mammies and their daddies and their fold-down chairs and their crisps and flags to cheer the marchers on, but me and Daisy stay in the house, mostly, and when we do go out, we stay in the garden. Sometimes we hide in the space between the biggest fir tree and the hedge and watch the people and the police vans in the street. The sun beats down on the marchers to the time of their own lambeg drums, and the heat makes everyone cross and cranky. But the two tall fir trees stand straight, never once drooping, even in the hottest times of the day, guarding our house from the road. The marching season is Daddy's busiest time at work. Some

3

nights, Daddy doesn't come home at all, and some days, he's up and out at the scrake of dawn, before me and Daisy are awake, even. Most of the time, when he gets home, he's too tired even to sing us a song. And these days, because Daddy comes home with the smell of the flutes and the fifes seeping off him, Mammy makes him sleep on the sofa.

The hot air is cracking with the sound of helicopters rack-a-tack-a-tack-a-tacking through it. Daddy says the helicopters have special cameras to see into houses so that the Army can watch what people are doing. Two helicopters hung above our street all afternoon and me and Daisy in the garden waved up at them but we couldn't see if anyone waved back at us. So we swung off the front gate and waved at the big grey Land-Rovers growling along our street with their mouths of steel like rows and rows of sharp teeth. Meatwagons: that's what Baps and Wee Man who live down our street call them. Daisy used to be scared of the Land-Rover meatwagons and me too a wee bit, though I said to Daisy I wasn't. Daddy says they're there to protect us but Mammy doesn't like them. Mammy saw us waving at them and she rushed out and slapped us both, even though it's Daisy's birthday.

—What do you think you're at, youse two?

—Sorry, Mammy.

—I'm after asking you a question! What do you think you're doing?

—We're sorry, Mammy.

—Don't sorry mammy me! How many times have I told you youse're not to be waving and being all friendly to the British Army vans?

The other children in our street wave at the Army vans. But I don't say anything.

—What if it's Daddy? Daisy says.

Sometimes Daddy drives a big grey Land-Rover but you can't see inside to see if it's him or not, so we wave at all the vans just in case.

—I don't care! I'm your mother and when you're in my house you do as I say and I don't want you waving at the British Army. They've no business to be installing themselves in this street and I won't have you waving at them.

Mammy makes us come inside and get bathed. She brushes our hair without getting the tangles out first and Daisy keeps crying. Then Mammy starts crying and she hugs us and keeps saying she's sorry.

We're watching at the window for Daddy coming home. Daisy keeps saying, When's Daddy coming home? and then she starts chanting, I'm hungry, I'm hung-gree, until Mammy loses her patience and shouts at us, for the second time on Daisy's birthday. Daddy promised to take us to JJ Bleekers to celebrate. Last time we went to JJ Bleekers was at Christmas and Mammy let us have Coke Floats and they came with pink flamingo swizzle-sticks and little paper umbrellas. For dessert there was Mississippi Mud Pie with whippy ice cream and chocolate ice cream both and you didn't have to choose which you'd rather and there were marshmallows as well. Daisy keeps gurning that she's hungry but she gurns even harder when Mammy takes a packet of fish fingers from the freezer and opens a can of baked beans.

—Blame your father, Mammy says as she spoons the baked beans out of the saucepan and sets the plates down on the table.

She hasn't made us change out of our party dresses. Mine is white with a ruffly skirt and a red-ribbon hem and red cherries printed all over it. Daisy's is pink with yellow spots and an orange blob where she spills baked beans over it because she's crying so hard. Mammy tied my hair with a red ribbon to match my dress, in a side-ponytail so that I could see the ribbon, and Daisy's is in a palm tree. Mammy took a picture of the two of us standing by the door in our best dresses holding hands.

—Smile, girls! Youse look beautiful.

Mammy looked beautiful too, but now she's frowning. She's still wearing her shiny pointy black shoes and her green dress that Daddy says matches her eyes. She sits at the kitchen table with us and finishes off the baked beans from the saucepan. Daisy won't let up wailing.

—Sure, and what do you expect me to do about it? Mammy says crossly. Blame your father, she says again. Then she says, Blame this bloody country.

We don't say anything. Mammy never swears.

Mammy is making us hot chocolate when Daddy gets home. She's cross; not at us any more we don't think, but we can tell she's cross at something because she's banging the mugs and milk is slopping out of them. She shakes in chocolate powder from the box and it puffs everywhere. Daddy stays leaning against the back door with his padded jacket over one arm. His face is grey and droopy.

—Get those boots off of you, Mammy goes, without turning round. I'm just after mopping the floor. She gives the two mugs of hot chocolate a final angry stir and carries them over to the table. There you go, girls. Mind, it's hot.

She runs the water in the sink and rinses the spoon. Then she picks up a teatowel and dries it and starts drying the plates on the draining board. Daddy is watching her. She still

doesn't turn around. Daddy comes up and hugs her around
the waist.

—Get off of me, she goes.

—I'm sorry, love, he goes.

—Sorry for what? She whirls around, hands on her hips.
Sorry for what exactly? Sorry for missing Daisy's birthday?
Sorry for breaking your promise to her? Sorry for this god-
forsaken hole we're living in?

—Calm down, love. There's been trouble up the Short
Strand.

—Calm down? *Calm down?* Don't you dare tell me to calm
down.

—I'm dead beat, love—

But Mammy interrupts him: Am I or am I not just after
asking you to take those dirty great boots off?

Daddy takes his boots off.

—Did you eat already? he asks.

—What do you think? Mammy goes. Ey? What do you
think? The girls were starved.

Daddy turns to us.

—I'm sorry, Daisy. I'm sorry, Sunshine. There was some
fighting, see, and Daddy couldn't get away. If there was any
way I could've been here I would've, you hear me?

We don't say anything.

—Can I take my girls to JJ Bleekers tomorrow night?

We nod. Mammy laughs, not a nice laugh.

—Are you sure you want to be making more promises
you'll not be keeping?

Daddy ignores her.

—Would you like a song? he goes.

—Yes please, says Daisy.

—It's too late and they're tired out, snaps Mammy. Finish

7

your hot chocolate, girls, and get upstairs. I'll be up to brush your teeth in a wee minute.

Daisy scampers on upstairs but I wait halfway and watch through the banisters.

—I'm sorry, Daddy goes. I kept thinking about the girls, and seeing their wee sad faces, but it got dead nasty at one point and—

—I don't want to hear about it.

—Love—

—I said I don't want to hear about it.

They stand facing each other for a moment, then Mammy turns away and starts crying. Her shoulders and back are shaking. Daddy strokes her hair and then he hugs her tight and this time she doesn't push him away.

—This can't go on, Mammy says.

Then she says, I can't go on like this.

—I know, Daddy says.

When Mammy comes up to brush our teeth and turn off the light, the helicopters are hanging overhead again, right above our house it seems, shuddering the night sky apart with their rack-a-tack-a-tack-a-tack, and the sound of sirens whines through the dull droning noise.

Mammy stares out of the window for a moment.

—Just ignore it, she says, tugging the curtains closed. Pretend you can't hear it.

—I can't pretend, Mammy.

—Of course you can! Pretend, just pretend you can't hear it and you'll soon be asleep.

—Can we have a story?

—Oh please, a story!

—No, girls, no story tonight.

—Please?

—Please?

—Pleasepleaseplease?

—I said no! It's too late tonight. Just get youse to sleep.

Mammy goes back downstairs. She hasn't tucked us in properly. So I tuck Daisy in, and she lies quietly for a bit, cuddling Emily and sucking Emily's woolly yellow plait. Then she goes, Sha-sha? That's how she says my name, Sha-sha, because she's too small to say it properly, *Seer-sha*, spelled ES-AY-OH-EYE-AR-ES-EE. Words are different in Irish than they are in English. Saoirse.

—Sha-sha? I can't sleep. Sing me a song!

I sing the one Daddy used to sing to me when I was smaller than Daisy. Daisy joins in with the uh-hum bits.

> —Oh Froggy went ah-kortin
> And he did ride
> Uh-hum uh-hum
> Oh Froggy went ah-kortin
> And he did ride
> Uh-hum uh-hum.

—What's ah-kortin? Daisy asks.

—Like swimming, I say. Like doggy-paddle.

Mammy is teaching me how to swim without armbands. If I hold on to the side of the swimming pool I can kick and kick and kick and almost let go. Mammy says soon I can go in the big pool all by myself: by the end of the summer, maybe. Daisy still has to wear orange armbands and her special blow-up ring that has ducks and daisies on it. But I don't need armbands any more.

Daisy wants the song about her as well. I can't remember

all of the words, so I sing, *Daisy, Daisy, give me your answer do* and she claps her hands and laughs and I have to tell her to shush because we're meant to be sleeping. But Daisy won't go to sleep. So I say I'll tell her a special birthday story.

—It's a story about a Princess, I go.

—What was her name? Was it Daisy?

—Yes. Princess Daisy.

—Was she beautiful?

—Oh yes, she was a right bobby-dazzler this Princess Daisy.

Daisy giggles. Bobby-dazzler is what Daddy calls Mammy when he's in a good mood.

—And she had a doll named Emily.

—See, Emily! Daisy shakes Emily. I hope you're listening carefully. The Princess had a doll called Emily, too.

—Shush. You have to close your eyes and listen.

Daisy squeezes her eyes shut and nods.

—Once-upon-a-time there was a Beautiful Princess who lived All Alone inside a Big Red Palace with only her Doll for Company, I begin. Daisy sighs and snuggles Emily tight. And before I'm even halfway into the story Daisy is fast asleep.

But I don't feel at all sleepy. I look at my ballerina box on the pillow next to me. The ballerina box is my favourite thing and it goes everywhere with me. It is covered in padded cream leather and it has a golden lock with a tiny key; the inside is lined with red velvet and when you open the lid a little white-and-gold ballerina with a tiny, stiff-net tutu springs up and pirouettes in front of a gilt-edged mirror. There is a golden button at the back of the box, and Mammy showed me how to turn it round and round until it's wound up fully and fairy music plays. Daisy is always wanting to touch the ballerina, but I never allow her because she's too little. I twist the button round and watch the ballerina turning and turning in front of the mirror, balancing on one leg, arms above her head. As the music starts to break down, she stops moving for a little bit, then, as the music gives one last splutter, she jerks back into a pirouette, and then she stops again.

Her music sounds sad sometimes. It sounds sad tonight. I close the lid, carefully.

2

The Shadow-Kings of the Otherworld are in need of mortal strength, and in their Assembly at the time of Samuin they mutter darkly about this growing need . . .

I can feel the Shadow-Kings creeping across the grass like a cold mist; feeling their way through the air with long, dark fingers; reaching for my ankles. I can almost see them out of the corner of my eye; almost, but not quite; and when I jump round, to take them by surprise, they're always gone.

I twirl round and round and round and round, as fast as I can, to confuse the shadows behind me. I twirl so quickly the garden tumbles upside down and flings me on to the grass with a bump.

Mammy laughs at me. Mammy is lying on the tartan rug spread out in the back garden, trying to get some colour. Mammy's skin is pale, and she wants to be tanned. But all that happens when she sunbathes is that she gets freckles across her nose and shoulders. Sometimes if Mammy's in a good mood she lets Daisy pretend to join up the freckles like a dot-to-dot book. Me and Daisy have freckles too, from playing outside so much. Mammy says freckles are marks where the sun has kissed you.

—When I was your age, Saoirse, all I wanted was to be a ballerina, Mammy goes, suddenly.

—Oh, I want to be a ballerina, I go, and the shadows melt away, and Mammy smiles at me and blows me a kiss.

—I was just like you when I was your age, she goes.

—Does that mean I'll look like you when I grow up? I ask. My mammy is the most beautiful lady in the whole of Belfast. Probably even in the whole of the world and the universe as well. Sometimes Daddy dances with Mammy right in the middle of the living room and he sings the song that he says was written for her: *She is handsome, she is pretty, she is the Belle of Belfast City.*

Mammy smiles again.

—Arenten I the luckiest mammy of them all, having two lovely wee daughters like the two of you.

I do a special twirl and curtsey. Mammy laughs and claps.

—Me too! Daisy squeals, hopping over to me and trying to do a curtsey too. Me too. I want to be a ballerina too!

—You can't be a ballerina, I go, once Mammy turns away.

—Why not?

—Because I bagsy ballerina first.

—Well, I'm going to be Queen of the Fairies then.

—You can't be a fairy. You're only a little girl. And you can't be Queen before I am, anyway.

—Can so. Every night me and Emily go to the Castle of Faery in Tir-nan-Og. We fly there, so we do.

I tell Daisy, you can't fly to Tir-nan-Og. It takes more than flying to get there. You need magic to get to Tir-nan-Og. And anyways, if you do go there, you can never ever come back because when you come back hundreds and hundreds of years have passed.

I check Mammy's not listening.

—If youse really had've gone to Tir-nan-Og, I whisper, you'd've turned to dust the minute you set foot on the soil and Mammy would've hoovered youse up by now.

—Mammy! Daisy gulders.

Mammy rolls over and blinks up at us.

—Are youse playing nicely now, girls?

—I want to be a ballerina too, Mammy, Daisy goes.

—Do you now.

—Like Sha-sha. I don't want to be dust.

—Dust?

—Sha-sha said. Like Tir-nan-Og.

—I'm sure she didn't mean it, Mammy goes. Then she goes, Do you girls want a story?

—Yes please, Mammy! I jump on to the rug beside her.

—Yes please! Daisy runs over with a fistful of daisies for Mammy to make into a necklace.

All summer, for our bedtime stories, Mammy has been telling us the tales of Cúchulainn. A couple of streets away from us, on the way to the leisure centre, is a wall with a painted picture of Cúchulainn and a sign saying 'Ancient Defender of Ulster against Irish Attacks'. Wee Man's big brother was one of the ones that did that painting. Me and Daisy asked Mammy what it meant. She said it was nonsense, for wasn't Cúchulainn himself Irish, for Ulster was part of Ireland in those days, before it got cut off. Mammy knows all about Cúchulainn. The tales she tells us are tales that she learned when she was a wee girl, she says. She says it's important that the stories are told. She's telling us the story of the Wasting Sickness of Cúchulainn, and of the Jealousy Bred between Fand and Emer-of-the-Yellow-Hair. Emer is Cúchulainn's sweetheart, but then Fand who came from Faery decided she loved Cúchulainn and poor Emer couldn't compete. Mammy's been telling us the story in bits at bedtime. It's a very sad story and me and Daisy can't wait for the ending to put things right again.

—Now, where did I leave off? she asks.

—After Cúchulainn fell down in a deep sleep and when

they found him and shook him he would only moan and his eyes were wild and rolling with longing!

—Well remembered! Mammy beams at me. Now, the Ulaid despaired, for even the mightiest of the druids couldn't say what would cure Cúchulainn of the Wasting Sickness. Because he was under the spell of the *Síde*, wasn't he? For those who dwell in the enchanted Castle of Faery had heard tell of Cúchulainn's strength and youth and bravery, and the Lady Fand, daughter of Aed Abrat, wife of Manandán, no longer loved her husband, and had decided to bestow her love upon Cúchulainn instead.

—Gifts of the *Síde* are dangerous, Mammy, arenten they, I go.

—Aye, pet, they're double-edged. You have to be careful with getting what you want because sometimes it turns out that when you've got it it'll destroy you. And the gift of love is the most dangerous of them all.

Mammy is quiet and her smile is wiped clean off her face.

—Mammy, I whisper.

—What? Where was I? she goes. Oh aye. The Lady Fand had decided to love Cúchulainn, the strongest of any man that ever lived, and the bravest, and—

—Not as brave as Daddy! Daisy goes. Not even Cúchulainn could fight my daddy, could he, Mammy? Could he?

—Shush, Daisy, I go. You mustn't interrupt. It's rude.

Mammy looks at Daisy with a funny look.

—When I first set eyes on your Daddy, Daisy-pet, I thought he was the strongest and bravest man I'd ever seen.

Daisy squirms with happiness.

—Go on, Mammy, I say. We need to know what happens next.

—Cúchulainn fell to his knees, weak and giddy with the

15

love of Fand – Fand, named after *the tear that covers the eye* –
and he could go no further. So he sent Lóeg, his loyal char-
ioteer, on the long journey to Tir-nan-Og, to bear the message
that Cúchulainn's life was at Fand's mercy. And when Lóeg
returned from Tir-nan-Og he—

Daisy suddenly squeals and puts her hands over her ears.

—What is it, pet? Mammy goes. What's the matter?

It's the dust. Daisy doesn't want to hear about Lóeg shriv-
elling up and turning to bits of dust.

Mammy thinks for a minute when I tell her why Daisy's
scared. Then she goes, It's all right, love, because Lóeg's under
the protection of the *Side*. He'll not turn to dust.

—You promise?

Mammy nods. Daisy looks at me and then she looks at
Mammy again.

—*Promise* promise?

—Oh, absolutely.

So Mammy goes on.

—Then straight away Cúchulainn sent Lóeg to speak to
Emer, and to bear a message to her: and the message was
that Cúchulainn's love for Emer was cold and dead as stone.
When Lóeg returned, Cúchulainn grabbed him and shook
him with the last of his strength and begged Lóeg to tell him
about the Lady Fand and Tir-nan-Og. He was like a sick man,
he was. Mammy pauses. Cúchulainn doesn't know, she
explains, that he is under a spell. He is enchanted by the
Otherworld, and enchanted by the love of Fand, and he is
going to betray Emer, and throw away everything that he has,
for a love which isn't love, for a love which is like a sickness,
a mist that descends and chokes reason. And yet, she says in
a soft, faraway voice, and yet, there's some say that the *Side*
cannot *make* you do anything; they can only prompt you to

do that which is already inside you. They can water the seed, but they cannot place the seed there in the first place.

I shiver, even under the hot sun. I can see the Shadow-Kings groping towards Cúchulainn, greedy for his mortal strength, and I can see Cúchulainn getting weaker and weaker as his own sick fevered mind destroys him.

—Cúchulainn drank in every word Lóeg uttered, says Mammy. There was utter silence in his courtyard, and the Assembly of Ulaid stood like statues, and the only noise was the sound of the light as it fell from the high window, hitting the polished buffalo horn which Cúchulainn carried at his side. And Cúchulainn smashed the horn, the better to hear Lóeg's words. In the land of the *Síde*, Lóeg said, there is a vat of mead, honey-wine brewed from clover and cooled with drops of dew untouched by the sun. You can dip and fill a goblet one hundred, two hundred – one thousand times, and still the vat remains full to the brim. There are trees that turn to gold and silver in the setting sun, and each day, every single tree bears fruit enough for a hundred men. 'Were it mine to give,' said Lóeg to his master, 'I would give this province, nay, this entire island, just to live for a day and a night in the land of the *Síde*.'

Mammy's voice, threading the story together, is tight and clear in the thick afternoon air.

—'O for one sip of a goblet of mead from that land,' Cúchulainn moaned. He writhed on the ground like a man crazed. 'O Lóeg, one sip from that goblet of mead will heal my heart and send the strength of old coursing through my veins. O for a goblet of mead from the land of the *Síde*—'

—A goblet of mead? I could be doing with one of them, says Daddy, who's come round the side of the house and into the back garden. He's walking heavily in his big black boots.

—Daddy! shouts Daisy, running and leaping up on to him to be tickled by his bristles. But Daddy winces and sets Daisy back on the ground without swinging her in the air like he usually does. And then we see that one side of Daddy's face is all puffed up.

—Jesus, are you all right? What's happened? says Mammy, standing up suddenly, dropping the daisy-chain necklace.

—It's nothing, love, says Daddy, frowning a tiny wee frown at Mammy. A blow to the jaw, that's all. They checked it out and A-OK'd me. But they've sent me home, to be on the safe side.

—Saoirse, go and get a packet of something frozen from the freezer, Mammy says. And fetch a teatowel. Now! Go!

I run and get a bag of sweetcorn. The ice burns my fingers, even when I hold it with the teatowel. Mammy's stroking the side of Daddy's face with the tips of her fingers.

—It's swelling up, she says. She takes the bag of sweetcorn from me and wraps the cloth around it and presses it to Daddy's cheek.

—It's all right, Daddy keeps saying. I'm grand. It's nothing. He takes Mammy's free hand and kisses the palm of it. Mammy takes a long shaky breath.

—Let's get you inside, she says gently, talking to Daddy like he's me or Daisy having a nightmare. That's an awful shock you gave me.

—What happened, Daddy? goes Daisy.

—Don't be bothering your father, Mammy goes quickly.

—It was just a wee accident, goes Daddy. Everything's grand. See? Daddy pulls a face at me and Daisy. Daisy giggles. Ouch, Daddy goes. Daisy giggles some more. But he meant it.

18

Mammy goes inside with Daddy. I try and finish the daisy-chain necklace for Daisy, but my fingers are too clumsy and they keep tearing the thin stems of the flowers.

Daddy lays down for a bit, and me and Daisy play quietly on the landing outside his bedroom waiting for him to feel better. We take it in turns to peek through the keyhole and see if he's awake. He wakes up in time for tea, but the side of his face has gone purple, and he can only smile out of one corner of his mouth. Daisy starts to cry when she sees Daddy's big purple face with only half a smile. But he catches her up and tickles her and then she starts laughing again. We all eat pizza together. Mammy says does Daddy want some chicken soup, with maybe a boiled spud in it, but Daddy says he's no invalid, and he eats pizza too, only he eats it in little sucky bites. Daisy and I have lemonade, and Daddy adds some beer to his and Mammy's lemonades to make shandies. We all clink glasses together.

—It's for good luck, Mammy explains. *Sláinte*, says Mammy.
—Bottoms up, says Daddy, and Daisy bursts out laughing at the rude word.

When Mammy tucks us into bed, I ask her to finish the story of the Wasting Sickness of Cúchulainn, but she says it's a story for another day.

—Please? I beg, scared for Cúchulainn, ill and under the spell of the *Síde*. Pleasepleaseplease?

—Tomorrow, Mammy says, but she sings one last song, the song that Emer-of-the-Yellow-Hair sings to Cúchulainn whom she loves and whose heart she knows is leaving her. Mammy sings it softly, like a lullaby, and her green eyes are big and dark and shining.

> —Alas! Blood my heart,
> wasting for the horseman of the plain.
> He comes not from Emuin –
> a spectre has parted us.

—Don't go, Mammy, I whisper, and she sings on.

> —See the onset of brilliant winter,
> see each wonder in turn;
> see then that which you serve,
> its coldness and distance and dimness.

—Emer gets Cúchulainn back in the end, doesn't she? I call. It'll spoil the story but I don't care.

Mammy turns in the doorway.

—Aye. In the end. Now sleep tight.

She blows me a kiss. Then she closes the bedroom door gently behind her.

3

Four houses down from us, Baps and Wee Man mix up mud to look like dog turd, and they leave it on our drive, just inside the gate. They'd come round looking for bits of fence or wood for the eleventh-night fires, and Mammy'd slammed the door on them so they're getting their own back on us. Baps has a soft, bready stomach that presses his loose shirt outwards; Wee Man has slanting eyes that are a pale yellow colour and a tight, pointy chin. Daisy and I are hiding in the space between the biggest fir tree and the hedge, waiting until they've gone.

They clang the gate shut behind them and give each other high fives up-above and down-below shouting: Beezer! Then they skulk around our bit of pavement for a bit waiting to see if anything happens. But there's not a peep out of me and Daisy crouching down behind the hedge, and Mammy's inside somewhere.

—Oyee, ye girl ye! goes Baps at a girl skipping just a bit along from them. She ignores him and starts to do cross-overs with the rope. I can't do cross-overs. Me and Daisy watch her flinging her arms wide to swing the rope then tucking them in and hunching her shoulders as the rope swishes over her head.

—Ye want it, don't ye? Baps persists. Ye want it! Baps laughs; a wet, gurgly noise.

—Go an' take yerself for a long walk off of a short bridge! the girl suddenly screeches back, and she runs off, trailing the skipping rope behind her.

Baps and Wee Man roar with laughter.

—Nice one! Wee Man goes. Nice one!

Later on, Baps and Wee Man and the girl that was skipping and another girl just a wee bit older than me dare each other to leave the dog turd mud right on our doorstep. Me and Daisy have been swinging in the back garden and Daisy hears the gate squeak and thinks it's Daddy come home. She runs round the front of the house and sees Wee Man crouching over the doorstep and Baps and the two girls swaying on the front gate and laughing. Mammy used to be friends with the girl my age's mammy for a bit. But when she came round or we went over there she used to make Secret Societies with me and say Daisy was too young to join them. And then Mammy said she didn't want us playing with the children on the street anyway. Daisy yells: Sha-sha! *Sha-sha!* And I come running and Wee Man legs it down the drive and the four of them take off down the street shouting: Taigs! Filthy stinking Ta-igs!

Mammy scrapes the mud off the doorstep and tells us to keep the gate closed and to play in the back garden. Her face is red and her eyes are shiny but she doesn't say anything except to say again that we're not to go out of the back garden; she doesn't even ask us if we know who put the dog turd mud there or why. The back garden's too small to play in; there's only the swing, and after a while I get bored pushing Daisy on it because she's too little to swing herself. Then when I start to swing she shouts that she wants a turn again. Hard cheese! I tell her. She had her go. And I don't get off the swing. I twist round and round until the rope's all tightly wound up, and then I push off the ground with my toes and the swing shudders and spins in tight, fast circles. Daisy keeps on screaming that it's her go even though she had a far longer turn than me. Then Mammy opens the window and gulders down that I'm not to do that for the ropes will fray and brake and for crying out loud will I let my wee sister have her go. It's so unfair, I say, but Mammy's gone from the window, and I don't want to make her cross, so I get off the swing and push Daisy on it until it's teatime.

Daddy says, from now on, for the Time Being, I'm not to cycle on the street. When I learned to ride without stabilizers I was allowed from our gate to the second lamppost, but now Daddy says I'm not to go out of our driveway. Daisy cycles around the little bit of lawn on her trike. But mine's a big girl's bike, without stabilizers now, and the garden's too small for me to cycle properly in. Mammy has told Daddy about the boys and girls from the street and the mud on our doorstep and the bad names and Daddy is going to have a word with their parents, he says. But in the meantime me and Daisy are to stay in the back garden and ignore them if we see them and they say anything. One afternoon when Daddy is at home he takes us up to Stormont so we can cycle down the hill. I go on ahead of Daddy and Daisy, and then cycle back down to them. Daddy tells me to keep both hands on the brakes as I am going down, for the hill's quare steep. I judder and bump down the first time, but the second time I am braver and the third time I am pretending my bike is a pony and I am cantering along. The wind squashes my face back and my forehead is sweaty under my pink My Little Pony cycling helmet. I stroke the handlebars of my bike and say, Gee-up, Starlight! If I ever have a pony its name is going to be Starlight. Daisy's is Cartwheels. I have to get off to push the bike back up the hill, and it takes a long time. Daddy and Daisy are playing on the grass at the top, and Daddy tells us about the family that used to live in Stormont before it became the Parliament Buildings. It was called Storm Mount in those days, before it got shortened. Like something out of a proper story. Daisy and I count twenty-seven windows and lose count. One family, and that whole big house all to themselves! We try counting the windows again, but this time we only get to twenty-two before we get muddled up.

It's getting late and Mammy will be wondering what's keeping us. Daddy gets up from the grass and stretches and lifts Daisy on to his shoulders. You can see all over Belfast from the top of the hill, and Daddy points out where our house is. You can't see our house exactly, but you can see Samson and Goliath, the two big yellow cranes in the Shipyard, and so you can guess roughly where our street is. Daisy waves.

On the way back home we stop at a newsagent's and buy ice lollies. Daddy buys the *Belfast Telegraph* as well but he doesn't read it, he only looks at the front page and then he shakes his head and folds it all up so you can't see the photos on the front. But I saw them. The pictures are of men dressed all in black with big black balaclavas pulled down over their faces and only little slits for their eyes. Some of the men are standing and some of the men are kneeling and all of the men are pointing their guns in the air. Mammy won't have the *Belfast Telegraph* in our house because she says there's never any new news in it. But I think maybe she's scared of the pictures, too.

We sit on a wall facing into the sun and eat our ice lollies. Daddy wipes our mouths with his hanky and says we mustn't let on to Mammy because she'll say we've spoiled our tea. He says we must eat every last bite of our tea and we mustn't say that we're not hungry, or else Mammy will have his guts for garters.

—Even if it's fish pie? I ask. Me and Daisy hate fish pie. Even with ketchup.

—Especially if it's fish pie. OK, Sunshine? You hear that, Daisy, you're to eat up all of your fish pie if it's fish pie for tea. If Mammy's gone to the trouble of making you your tea you have to eat it all up, every mouthful. Is that understood, both of youse?

We hate fish pie so much. Daddy's frowning.

—Yes, Daddy, I go, without looking at Daisy.

—Yes, Daddy, Daisy goes.

—That's my girls.

Then Daddy gives Daisy a piggy-back the rest of the way, and he carries her trike under one arm. He says that if the weather holds we can go cycling up Stormont another time, and have another ice lolly afterwards. But he's away a lot, and my poor Starlight has to stay in the garage for the rest of the summer because Daddy still says I'm not to go out in the street. Sorry, Sunshine, he says, and he taps the end of my nose. Sorry, Sunshine, but it's best if you stay in the garden. I don't want you mixing up in any trouble.

He says he'll buy us a bigger swing for the back garden, one with two swings and a see-saw swing as well so we can both swing at once, but he never gets round to digging up the vegetable patch to make room for it.

There'll be nowhere to play properly now that we can't play in the street. The garden is too small to run about in, and Daddy's once-upon-a-time vegetable patch takes up most of the room. Last spring, he cleared all the shrubs from the scrubby bit of land beside the old oil tank, and decided that a vegetable patch could be Mammy's Project, to get her outside in the fresh air and put Roses In Her Cheeks. He brought home bags of special soil, and mixed it up with smelly greeny brown liquid, and dug it all into the earth, and I helped him plant lettuces, and carrots, and potatoes, and rhubarb along the wall, and we pretended that Daisy was helping too although she was far too little and just toddled about picking up handfuls of dirt. Then every day for days and days we would rush outside to see if it had all grown yet. Daddy told us that plants like it if you talk to them, so we sat and told stories to the soil until a coating of fluffy green appeared on the surface, and then little shoots started to poke through. We watered them in the morning and in the evening, filling up the rusty watering can from the tap at the side of the garage, both of us lugging it over to the vegetable patch and splashing the water out on to the earth. When the plants got big, Daddy said it was serious, and we had to start weeding else the weeds would take over and suffocate the poor baby vegetables. For a couple of weeks Mammy weeded with us, telling us what was a weed and what wasn't, but she got bored of it because it made her hot and dirty and it made her back hurt and she hadn't spent most of her life dreaming of getting away to end up growing vegetables again. It was all right for our daddy to dream up ridiculous schemes but he wasn't there half the time and he just left it up to other people to do the dirty work. Mammy kept on asking what we were going to do with a load of mangy auld lettuces and six rows of carrots. Daisy and I hoped she'd buy us a rabbit. But after a while everyone forgot about the vegetable patch, and for a little bit Daisy and I did try and weed but we couldn't remember which ones were the baby vegetables. In the end buttercups grew there, and pretty spindly white flowers, and puffy dandelion-balls that told you the a'clock by how many times you blew them.

For two weeks in spring, we spent all our time collecting caterpillars from the vegetable patch. Mammy punched holes in the lid of a jam jar, and we put little pebbles and grass and sticks inside, and that's where we kept the caterpillars, watching for them to turn into butterflies. Daisy lost me my best ever caterpillar. He was big and fat and brown, with horns and spiky hairs all along his back. He moved around fast, bunching himself up in the middle and sometimes standing on his tail and waving his front end around in the air, curling his horns at us. We watched him crawling round and round the sides of the jam jar. Then Daisy found another caterpillar, a wee tiny thin bright green one, but she didn't want to put him in the jam jar because he was so small and the other one was so big and fast and angry. Mammy found her a matchbox to put it in. Daisy said the matchbox wasn't big enough, but Mammy said for goodness' sakes it was only a little caterpillar. I put a leaf and some grass in the matchbox to make it more comfortable, but Daisy said her poor wee caterpillar would be scared in the dark. After dinner she wouldn't come out and play with me, but it wasn't until we went to bed that I realized my ballerina box was missing. I couldn't sleep without it, and I cried and cried until Mammy found it under Daisy's bed. Daisy had made a miniature garden inside, filling it with earth and twigs and leaves, and there were dirty smeary streaks across the red velvet. Mammy slapped Daisy across the back of the legs, and said Daisy should thank her lucky stars Daddy wasn't home or he'd give her a hiding she'd never forget. Mammy threw the caterpillar and all of the earth and leaves out the window, and she made me empty the horned caterpillar out of the jar, too, and I had to show her the jar to be sure I'd done it and she said that she'd had enough and we weren't to collect caterpillars again.

—But we want to see how the magic works!

—There's no magic, it's just Nature. Now get youse to bed, and there's not to be another peep out of either of youse or you'll be sorry!

I lay awake in my bed, thinking of the poor little caterpillars just thrown on to the gravel, not even near any bushes; and I thought of the poor little ballerina being shut in a dirty box with the caterpillar slithering towards her, because although it was only wee it must've seemed like a big serpent to her.

Daisy was awake too. After a while she whispered could she come and share my bed because she didn't like the dark, but I pretended to be asleep. Then she asked again, and when I didn't answer she padded across the floor and squeezed in beside me. I shuffled in the bed to push her to the very edge, but she didn't complain about it, and just lay there sucking her thumb until I let her have some of the duvet and we both fell asleep.

Mammy's taken to her bed when we get back from our cycle, so we don't have to eat fish pie for tea after all. Daddy makes us egg beat up in a cup with toast soldiers and he lets us have as much ketchup as we want instead of just one blob on the side of the plate. Then as soon as tea's over he says we must be tired after such a long ride so we'd best get on up to bed, but it's still so sunny outside and we're not really tired at all, so we watch from our bedroom window in case Baps and Wee Man and the others try and put any more dog turd mud on our doorstep. We watch until the street lights start to go on, and Daisy points at the little red lights in the sky and says they're the Enchanted Castle of Faery.

—No they're not, I go, they're the lights on helicopters and things.

—Are not.

—Are so! I'm bigger than you so I should know.

But Daisy insists that the lights are the lights of Faery. She says she knows the way there, but it's a secret and she's not allowed to tell. Then we hear Daddy coming up the stairs so we scurry to bed.

4

Daisy's Inner Ear has come back. If you talk to her, sometimes she doesn't hear what you're saying, and when Mammy shines a torch and looks, her ear is all gluey. Daisy had an Inner Ear at the beginning of the summer, and we had to go to the nurse at the health clinic and get special eardrops. When you look at Daisy's ears from the outside, they look perfectly normal. But that's what the nurse at the clinic said: she's got an Inner Ear. There are still some eardrops left. Mammy makes Daisy lie on the sofa and she drops the drops in Daisy's normal ear and I help her count how many she's put in. Daisy wriggles and cries and says it feels cold.

—Keep still! Mammy goes. But Daisy's good ear is pressed against the sofa and she probably can't hear Mammy because she wriggles even harder. It's funny that having an extra ear makes you deaf, I think. I poke my fingers as far as possible in my ears to check there's not another one growing in there. Mammy sees me and laughs and says I'm not to be silly. But I worry, all the same.

One morning, Mammy pours orange juice over our Shreddies. There's no milk been delivered, she says. There're no milk deliveries because there's no more milk bottles to put the milk in, I tell Daisy. We saw the news, after Children's BBC, and they showed wee boys chucking milk bottles and bricks at a row of Army vans. There were cars burning in the background, and big piles of wooden crates and fencing and barbed wire. Mammy came in and turned the television off. That's quite enough TV for one day, she said. But we didn't complain because then she did a jigsaw puzzle with us, a proper grown-up one, spreading the pieces all over the living-room floor. She showed us how to start with the ground and the sky, finding all of the pieces with a flat edge. It was Daisy's job to find all the pieces with a bit of blue sky on them, and Mammy and I fitted them together. The jigsaw was a jungle scene, with tigers and monkeys and parrots, and she let us leave it on the floor so that Daddy could see it when he came in.

Me and Daisy like it that there's no more milk because orange juice on Shreddies is more fun, but Mammy doesn't like it because you can't put orange juice in coffee. Is it too much to ask, she says, to have a wee drop of milk for your coffee? Is it too much to ask?

When we walk to the shops to buy milk, we see where they burned a car at the bottom of our street a few nights ago. Twisted black bones are all that is left of the car. The ground is smooth and shiny all around, where the road melted in the heat of the flames.

Daddy says that for the foreseeable future, while there're cars being burned and milk bottles being thrown, Mammy is not to take us across town to visit the Antoney-oney-os and their ice-cream parlour. He says that if Mammy wants to see her friends they can come to our house. He isn't cross when he says it. He says In Light Of Circ-um-stances. Me and Daisy aren't sure what Circ-um-stances are. I think he means the two of us. Mammy gets cross. And she doesn't like it when Daddy calls them the Antoney-oney-os.

—It's not funny. In fact, it's downright bigotry, so it is. You're just a pig-headed bigot.

31

—Jesus, woman! Catch yourself on! It's only my wee joke.

—A wee joke, is it? Well, do you see me laughing? Some joke! I don't think it's a joke, snaps Mammy. Then she adds, I think it's just damn rude.

Daddy doesn't like being called Damn Rude.

—Oho, well, talking of damn rude, it seems to me that those so-called friends of yours are damn rude. Explain to me again why it is that it's always you trailing the girls over there to visit them? What kind of friends will never come round to our house, ey?

—You know fine rightly why they won't come over this side of town.

—Well, in that case you'll understand fine rightly why I won't have you taking the girls over that side of town. Not until things calm down.

Mammy rolls her eyes but she doesn't say anything, like that's the end of it. But she still takes us to visit the Antoney-oney-os (only I'm not allowed to call them that or I'll get a slap across the back of the legs) but it's a Secret we're not to tell Daddy. I'm glad we don't have to stop our visits to the ice-cream parlour. We have to get two buses to get there, a bus into town that takes us to the City Hall and then we have to walk round the back of Leisureworld and get another bus up the Falls. The bus that goes up the Falls has metal mesh across the windows, just in case anyone throws a stone, Mammy says. Daisy and I press our noses right up against the glass to try and see out of the metal mesh. Sometimes you can only see mesh, and then your eyes pop and you can see outside until they pop again and you can't see past the metal. The ice-cream parlour is called An-to-ni-nis' Ices. That's how you say their name properly: An-to-ni-ni. Mr An-to-ni-ni – Grandpa Tony, he tells us to call him – makes me a special ice cream in a tall glass, with vanilla *and* strawberry ice cream and chocolate sauce *and* marshmallows and whippy cream and he never forgets to put a bright red cherry on top that I save till last. Sometimes he sticks a little paper umbrella in the whippy cream, and I lick the stick and fold it down and put it carefully in the pocket of my pinafore. I keep the paper umbrellas in the ballerina box with my other treasures. When Grandpa Tony sets the ice–cream sundae on the counter in front of me, Mammy opens her eyes wide and says, Heavens above, and aren't you the lucky girl? Have you said thank you to Mr Antonini?

—Ah, it's Grandpa Tony, he says, and he does a little bow and presents me with a long silver spoon. Da-dah! There you are, my *principessa*.

He turns to Mammy, shaking his head and pretending to be angry.

—And your Mama, we need to feed her up, eh? Too skinny, you hear me? You're too skinny, he tells her.

Mammy smiles a tight little smile and turns away.

—I'm just a wee bit tired these days, she goes.

Mammy and Isabella, Mammy's best friend, drink little cups of coffee like dolls' cups. Me and Daisy sit on stools up at the shiny counter and eat our ice creams with our spoons that have long handles so you can reach right into the bottom of the glass. Isabella's baby Andrea is strapped in a high chair beside us. Andrea is a baby boy. There's two girls in my class at school called Andrea. But Mammy says that in Italy, Andrea is a boy's name. Baby Andrea is fat, with squashy cheeks and lots of curly black hair. Sometimes, if we go to Isabella's house instead of the ice-cream parlour, me and Daisy have to play with Baby Andrea. Isabella gives us crayons and a colouring-in book, but if Andrea scribbles over our pictures or snaps a wax crayon in half we mustn't say anything because he's not our brother and we're guests in Isabella's house. Mammy tells me to be a good girl and play nicely with Andrea, and Isabella says to Andrea we're his Irish sisters, and I can't say that me and Daisy don't want to play with the baby. And to make things even worse Isabella's house doesn't have a garden to play in. The front door opens right on to the pavement, and we're not allowed to play in the street even though there're always other children playing out there. I said to Mammy why can't Isabella and Andrea come over and play in our house that has a garden, but Mammy says that Isabella is scared to come to our part of town because she's from a foreign family and some people in some parts of Belfast don't like people from other countries. When she says that I think of Baps and Wee Man and sometimes the girls on our street yelling, Away back to yer own country, ya Taig! and, Tell your ma she's not welcome here! But I don't tell Mammy that.

The An-to-ni-nis come from a little village in the mountains called Cassylahteeko.

—Cassylahteeko! goes Grandpa Tony.

—Cassy-LAH-teeko! I say, and he laughs, and makes his happy-clown face.

Grandpa Tony has pictures of Cassylahteeko on the walls of the ice-cream parlour, and sometimes he points out his house. It's small and white, with a roof made out of tiles, and a pig and a chicken sitting outside. Cassylahteeko is in Italy. Mammy showed me Italy in the map of the world in our encyclopaedia. But we couldn't find Cassylahteeko. I told Grandpa Tony that, and his face went all droopy.

—All the people leave, he said. All the people want better life.

—Why'd'ye come to Ireland then? I said. Grandpa Tony's always going on about how beautiful Italy is and how sunny Italy is. Italy sounds far better. In Ireland it just rains all the time and when it is hot the people get mad.

—When you grow up, *principessa*, you leave this country and you go to live with my family, *capisci*? Marry a nice Italian boy, no? You're gonna be a heartbreaker, *bellissima* just like your mama, and I tell you all the Italian boys gonna be falling over themselves to marry you!

Grandpa Tony has started teaching me some Italian words for when I go to his house in Italy and marry an Italian boy. But I'm not sure if I want to go to Italy because even if it is better than Ireland and even if I could have a proper big Italian ice cream every day like he says I'd miss Mammy and Daddy and Daisy. I whisper that in Mammy's ear and she kisses me and says, not to worry, he's just Home-Sick and it makes him feel better talking about Italy.

Home-Sick is a special kind of sick you get when you're away from your home. It's not like a tummy-bug because you get it by just thinking about people or places and the only cure is to go back home.

—Why doesn't he go back home then?

Mammy sighs.

Perhaps he'll turn to dust, I think, the minute his foot touches the soil.

—A long time ago, before you were born, *céadsearc*, there was a war, and lots of people left Italy to come to Ireland. Grandpa Tony was one of those people, and his home is here, now.

—Well, why does he get Home-Sick then? I interrupt.

—Oh, Sha. Isabella – Grandpa Tony's her daddy – she was born here, and she grew up here and married a man from

35

here, and wee babby Andrea will grow up here, and they're Grandpa Tony's family. But sometimes, Grandpa Tony gets sad about everything he left behind.

I still don't understand why he can't go home just for a little bit, just until the Home-Sick wears off, but Mammy says that even if he went back, nothing would be how he remembered it, and maybe the home he left all those years ago wouldn't be there any more.

Mammy goes quiet and her eyes go all shiny.

—Why are you crying, Mammy? I whisper.

—I'm not crying, she goes, and she turns away. But I saw a tear slide down her cheek and drip off the end of her chin and she didn't even brush it away.

The air is thick with heat and sweat and me and Daisy are bored playing in the back garden. My hair is damp across my forehead and my skin is all crawly and itchy. The girl across the road has a paddling pool in her front garden and some other girls from our street are playing in it, but Mammy's said we're to stay away from them after the dog turd mud. I don't want to play with them anyway. Yer eyes are too close thegether, they've started shouting when they see me and Daisy. My eyes don't look too close together to me. But it's hard to tell. I look at Daisy's eyes; hers don't either. But I can't tell how close is too close.

Daisy and I want an ice cream. We ask Daddy if we can go to the shop at the bottom of the road. Daddy was working all last night so he's sitting in a chair in the garden, snoring, with the *East Belfast Newsletter* over his head. We take it in turns to poke him until he wakes up with a jolt. He says he doesn't want us going to the shop. Please, Daddy! we go, but he still says no. Please will you come with us, we say, but he says he's dead beat and will we ever give his head peace. In the end he gets us each an Ice Pop from the freezer but there's only the blue ones left and we don't like the blue ones. They have a funny taste. I like the red ones and the green ones and Daisy likes the yellow ones and the orange ones, and we both like the pink ones, but neither of us likes the blue ones. Daisy throws her blue Ice Pop on the kitchen floor and Daddy shouts.

—Daisy! Pick it up this instant!

—No! I want a proper ice cream! Like Grandpa Tony makes! I want to go to Grandpa Tony's!

We're not supposed to mention one word about going to see Grandpa Tony because it's a Secret. Daisy remembers as soon as she's said it and she goes quiet and looks at me all big-eyed.

—Has your mother been taking you to that ice-cream parlour?

Daisy looks at me and I look at Daisy and then I look down at my sandals and fit my feet along the cracks in the kitchen tiles. Daisy's blue Ice Pop is melting on the floor. Mine is melting too and it's dripping down my hand. My hand is cold where I'm holding the Ice Pop. There's a different sort of cold, as well, in the middle of my tummy.

—Sunshine? Answer me.

I still don't say anything. The cold patch in my tummy is getting bigger.

—Sunshine! Look at me when I'm talking to you!

Daddy's guldering. A bit of spit goes on my cheek. I wipe it off with my gooey blue hand and leave a sticky cold smear on my cheek.

—Sunshine! he roars. I'm your father! If I ask you a question you're to answer!

37

—Yes, Daddy, I whisper.

—What do you mean: *Yes, Daddy*? Has your mother been taking you to that ice-cream place?

—Yes, Daddy, I say again.

Mammy's in bed with one of her sore heads but it doesn't stop Daddy storming up the stairs and shouting at the top of his voice.

—Daddy's ragin', I say to Daisy. That's your fault, so it is.

—No, she says, scared.

—It is, I go.

We don't get to go to the ice-cream parlour again. One day, Mammy puts down the phone white as a sheet, and she pushes me away when I try and hug her, and she says that Isabella and Baby Andrea and Grandpa Tony are going back to Italy for good. We take two taxis to Isabella's house in the Falls, one normal taxi and one big black taxi, because the big black taxis are the only ones that will go up the Falls. Isabella's tiny wee house is full of people, and more and more people are coming and going all the time, bringing casserole dishes of food and making tea and smoking and crying and talking in angry whispers, and I watch behind the blinds as a big van with BBC on it films the house and the street until a woman in a padded pink coat with rollers in her hair still comes up and tugs the blinds back down and pulls me away and says, It's a disgrace, so it is, coming to juke at us like we're animals in a zoo, they've no respect, so they haven't, no respect at all.

So then I sit in a corner, cross-legged and quiet, shushing Daisy when she starts to play too noisily. Mammy starts to cry, and she and Isabella hug each other, and Mammy seizes Baby Andrea on to her lap and kisses him again and again and says, You poor wee thing, you poor, poor wee thing, until Andrea starts gurning too.

Later on that evening, crouching on the little landing halfway up the stairs and pressing my face in the gap between two of the banisters, I can see a slice of the living room and hear Mammy and Daddy talking about what happened to Isabella's husband Frankie.

—He's sitting at the bar, Mammy goes, just sitting having a quiet wee drink, after work, like. Just sitting on his tod having a quiet wee drink.

—Aye, I know, says Daddy. Terrible shame, so it is.

—A *shame*? Is that what you call it? Jesus, a shame?

—Look, love, Daddy interrupts, this isn't helping anything, but Mammy will not be talked down.

—Them two Loyalist gunmen burst out of the bogs with their ballyclavas and their machine guns, burst out and start shooting all around them—

—Calm down, love—

—And you call it a *shame*?

—Love—

—Jesus.

—There's no need for this! You're getting yourself worked up. There's nothing to be done.

Mammy ignores him and raises her voice again.

—Frankie's his back to them. And do you know what?

Daddy's shoulders slump and he sits down.

—*Do you know what?*

Mammy's voice is shrill and her face is twisted so it doesn't look like Mammy any more. I want to go back to bed. I want to go back to bed and climb in with Daisy. But I can't even stop looking.

—What, love?

—They said his neck was almost completely blown away. His head was barely attached to his body. Isabella had to . . . had to identify him and his head was barely attached to his . . . And Isabella's had to hear all the details again and again from the police and on the telly and on the radio and – What kind of country are we living in, can you tell me that? Jesus, what kind of life is this? Why did I ever come up North? What possessed me, for crying out loud?

Daddy's got up and he's grabbing her wrists and she's shrieking. I cover my ears with my hands. But I can't move from where I'm crouched down on the stairs looking through the banisters. When I take my hands from my ears, I hear Daddy saying how the brother of one of the gunmen was in the Forces and how that brother and that brother's wife were blown up by a bomb planted underneath their car, blown up in front of their six-year-old daughter and the babysitter, who were waving bye-bye from the front room.

—Sunshine's age! That wee girl was no older than our Sunshine.

—Are you – are you *justifying* what those men done?

—I'm not justifying. Jesus! I'm not – justifying, I'm only saying.

—I cannot believe I'm hearing this. No, get off of me! I cannot believe you're justifying what those men done. Think of that wee baby boy with no father. Think of—

Daddy's shouting over her now.

—What I think of is I think of that wee girl who saw her mummy and daddy killed – blown up – in front of her. That the wee girl is the exact same age as my Sunshine.

—You're disgusting, so you are. Bringing my children into this to use against me.

—That's not what I'm doing, I'm only saying—

—So what are you saying?

—What I'm saying, is—

—What you're saying is that it's all right for men to go into a pub and kill innocent men like Frankie? That revenge is all right so long as it's avenging something terrible enough?

—Jesus, that's not what I'm saying. I'm just saying . . . there's always more to it. That's what I'm saying. Catholic Men Shot Dead in Pub by Loyalist Paramilitaries, the headlines go. But the story behind it . . .

Mammy's gone all quiet and staring.

—I don't believe I know you, so I don't.

—Come on, love. All I'm saying is that it fucking terrifies me, what goes on. He reaches out to touch her hair.

—Don't! Don't you dare touch me! Mammy's crying and gulping and shaking. What's become of us? she says, over and over again. What's become of us? What have we done?

I creep upstairs to bed, and get into Daisy's bed. Daisy is milky-warm and smells of sleep, but I am shivering and my ears are ringing with the harsh sound of bombs and guns and ballyclavas and whenever I close my eyes I see floating in front of me that little girl my age's face as she waves from the front-room window.

The next morning, when me and Daisy go downstairs, Daddy is sleeping on the sofa.

—Sha-sha, why does Daddy like sleeping on the sofa? Daisy asks.

I tell her to shush. But Daddy wakes up.

—What are you girls doing up so early? he says.

—It's not early, Daddy, it's breakfast time, Daisy goes.

—Breakfast time, already? Daddy goes, pretending to be

shocked. Sure, it wasn't that long ago I went to bed, it can't be *breakfast* time!.

There's purple under Daddy's eyes that looks like me or Daisy crayoned it in with colouring pencil, and his eyes are small and pink and puffy like the eyes of the school rabbit when it got sick. Daddy looks at me with a funny look on his face. Then he yawns and stretches and does his monkey impression. Daisy giggles.

—Come on, girls, he goes, and Daisy jumps on to his lap. I slide in beside him on the sofa, and he puts an arm round me. Listen to me carefully, he goes. I don't know what you may have heard people saying the past couple of days, but you're not to be scared and you're to remember that your daddy will always protect you, d'ye hear me? Ey?

He's gripping my arm, and he looks fierce. I nod. Daisy nods too, wide-eyed.

—Never you forget that it's your daddy's job to protect people, and to catch the bad people and make sure they go to jail. Understand? So long as I'm here, nothing will hurt you. Ey? You with me? Nothing will hurt you. You girls remember that, now.

—OK, Daddy, I whisper.

—Give me a kiss. Now let's get up and dressed and get some breakfast in the both of youse.

5

The coldness sits in my tummy like a lump of ice and every time I start to fall asleep I see a man from behind, and he's turning, slowly slowly turning, and I know that when he faces me his head will flop off his neck, where it's only attached by a single strip of skin. Mammy's not left the landing light on tonight, and the only light is the fuzzy orange of the street-light, coming in through the gap where the curtains don't close properly. Daisy's asleep, her mouth open, squashing Emily against her pillow and dribbling on one of Emily's plaits.

—Daisy, I whisper. Wake up!

But Daisy's fast asleep. There are spiky shadows on the walls, and they look like twisty witches' arms with spindly fingers, scrabbling at the poster that we saved up tokens and Mammy sent away for from Shreddies. I slip out of bed and scurry down the landing to Mammy and Daddy's room. The light is on, and the door is open a wee bit.

—Mammy?

—Who's that?

—It's me, Mammy.

She's sitting in the bed with her arms around her knees and the duvet over her shoulders.

—Mammy?

She blinks, and turns around slowly.

—It's late, love. Did I not put you to bed yet?

—Yes, Mammy.

—Get back to bed then.

—Mammy please, a story, Mammy?

She sighs.

—Can you not sleep either? All right. C'mere, pet.

I clamber into Mammy's bed and snuggle up against her. She hugs me tight, cramming my head against her shoulder so that I breathe in mouthfuls of her hair.

—Where's Daddy, Mammy? Is he on nights the night?

She crams me tighter like she wants to press me right inside her.

—Oh, *céadsearc*, my poor wee love, my beautiful wee girl.

Then, suddenly, she lets go of me and straightens my old pink pyjama top and picks a few balls off it.

—You need new pyjamas, love.

—I know, Mammy.

—These ones are far too small for you. You're shooting up this summer. Aye, you'll need new ones right enough. We'll have to go to C&A.

—I'm sorry, Mammy.

—What? Don't be silly, pet, she says, vaguely. Then she says, You want a story?

—Yes please, Mammy.

—What story do you want?

—Can I have Deirdre of the Sorrows? I go. *Though you will have fame and beauty, Deirdre, you will destroy all that you love and all who love you.* I'm never, ever, ever tired of hearing that story.

—Ach no, pet, not that one. Not tonight. Choose another.

I wish she would tell the story of Cúchulainn and the Cattle Rais, the *Táin Bó Cúailnge.* Or the story of the wooing of Étaín. Mammy is teaching us how to say Irish so we can understand the names.

—Would you like Sleeping Beauty? Mammy offers, before

44

I've made up my mind which story to ask for. Sleeping Beauty's a good story for bedtime, she adds.

I want a Cúchulainn story. But I nod.

—A long, long time ago, when the High King's minstrels at Emain Macha had not the half of the stories they were to sing about in times to come, there was a beautiful girl, a Princess.

—What did she look like, Mammy?

—She had smooth skin of ivory, and sparkling eyes of emerald that glittered like the Isle itself, so they said.

—What about her hair, Mammy? Was it black like mine?

—Aye, black like mine and like yours, pet, hair of jet black silk she had, our Princess, hair that fell over her shoulders and down her back like a rush of water. Men came to the palace for miles and miles around desperate to catch a glimpse of the Princess. And every night there was feasting and dancing, and the harpists and balladeers would play and sing songs that made their listeners' ears bleed, melodies that would have melted the hearts of the Mountains of Mourne.

Mammy's voice is soft and low and syrupy. I snuggle up to her some more.

—Tell me about the feast, Mammy.

Every time she tells the story, Mammy makes up more and more dishes for the banquet. Daddy says that no matter how much he's eaten for tea, he gets hungry all over again hearing Mammy describing the fairy-story banquets.

—Well, pet, the banquet dishes would be spread on white, lavender-scented cloths: sliver platters heaped with candied pear patina and damsons soaked in rose honey, exotic fruits like stargazers and jujubes, their skins warmed by the suns of far-off lands . . .

—What else, Mammy, what else?

—Jellies made with milk-fattened snails and sprinkled with hyssop and dill, little cinnamon-dusted cakes baked with the blood of day-old cygnets, the smoked knuckles of a thousand piglets seared in the fat of geese and dripping hot, figpecker birds fattened on truffle-oil and drowned in vats of red wine – can you imagine? Baby turtle doves roasted in bitter chocolate until the meat slipped from the bones at the slightest flicker of your tongue . . .

I don't like the food Mammy's making up this time. But she's hurtling on again before I can say anything.

—But beyond all of this merriment some great, unspeakable sadness lurked, and it lingered and clung in corners, pooling like mist in the spaces that people left behind as they turned their backs, and this despite the efforts of the King and the Queen to banish it, or at least to hide it with colour and music and laughter and light. For at their daughter's birth strange omens had been foretold. Some piglets born that day had tails and trotters sprouting from their mouths, so that they could not suckle. Cows trampled their shrieking young to death, and hunting dogs, pure-bred bitches who were reliable breeders many times over, howled and snarled and, mouths foaming, tore apart their puppies, their mewling, blind, pawing puppies.

—No, Mammy, I whisper, and my throat's so dry it comes out like a croak. Stop now.

But she doesn't hear me. And I don't think she could stop even if she wanted to. The story is whirling her along with it, and her voice is low and hoarse.

—And then, one day, years later, something happened to the Princess as she was walking alone through the palace. She pricked her finger – on a splinter, perhaps, or a shard of glass – and she fell drowsy to the ground, and lay sleeping on the cool stone floor of an upper room in the north wing, and when she woke up the palace and all its beauty and her childhood life were nothing but a hazy dream, a fantastic story, which later she would tell herself over and over with wonder, and with a sickness in her stomach.

There is a long silence.

It's getting light outside, and I can hear the cheeping of the first birds. Mammy's closed her eyes, and she's leaning back against the padded headboard, as if she's fallen asleep. But then she rubs her hands across her face, and she opens her eyes, and then she looks at me, and she looks scareder than I've ever seen anyone look ever, and she whispers, Jesus, O Jesus, O Mary Mother of God have mercy, and she reaches out to stroke the hair from my forehead and I try to duck away but her hands brush against me and they're trembling and sweaty and cold.

When Mammy is ill Daddy makes her hottoddy with sugar and cloves. But Daddy isn't here any more – he's gone away for a while, Mammy says, and she says would we ever give her head peace and not keep on plaguing her about when he'll be back because she doesn't know – and Mammy's just lying in bed, staring up at the ceiling, not moving, and she won't talk to us when we ask her what's the matter. Daisy and I empty the toys out of the toy box and I turn it upside down and climb on top of it to reach the very top kitchen cupboard. I find the whiskey bottle and pour out a full glass. I pour carefully but it still splashes a bit and Daisy says it smells nasty.

—It's medicine, that's why.

—I like pink medicine better. Why doesn't Mammy want pink medicine?

When me or Daisy can't sleep or if we have a cough Mammy gives us a spoon of Tixylix. Tixylix tastes like strawberry sweets and when you breathe it's like you can breathe fire like dragons do. But grown-ups need different medicine than little girls.

—Can I have a spoon of pink medicine? Daisy goes.

—No, because you're not sick.

I put the bottle back carefully and close the cupboard and slide down off the kitchen counter and wipe my hands on my T-shirt.

—I think my tummy's sore, Daisy goes.

—No it's not. We have to make hottoddy for Mammy.

Daisy gets the bag of sugar and I get the plastic tub of cloves. At Christmas Mammy showed us how to push lots and lots of cloves into an orange until there wasn't any more orange to be seen. Then we tied a purple ribbon around the clove-orange and put it in the airing cupboard at the end of the landing until it was all dried out. It made my and Daisy's face-cloths and bath towels smell all spicy. We gave it to Grandpa Tony for a Christmas present to say thank you for all of our special ice creams that he made us. Daisy wants to make another clove-orange now but there're no oranges. She says, Why don't we use an apple? But I tell her the cloves are for if Mammy needs a hottoddy. The tub's nearly empty now and we mustn't use them all up. Hottoddies are meant to be hot but we're not allowed to lay a finger on the stove. I think I've seen Daddy adding boiling water but we're not allowed to use the kettle either. So I stir the whiskey and sugar and cloves all together and let Daisy have a go as well. Then I carry it up the stairs to Mammy's room, carefully, with both hands, because it's full to the brim. I don't spill a single drop. Mammy's still just lying in bed and she doesn't say anything even when I say I've made her a hottoddy. I pat her cheek and try and help her drink but her face is loose and her mouth is drooping open and it just dribbles out and into her hair and then she turns away to face the wall. I put the glass on her bedside table for when she's feeling better and I tiptoe back downstairs.

Later on there is a crash and I make Daisy stay on the halfway landing while I see if Mammy's all right. The door's open a little bit and I can see a light brown hottoddy stain on the wallpaper and bits of glass and mess and sick on the carpet. Mammy is sitting on the orange rug on the floor at the foot of the bed with her head buried in between her knees and she's sort of rocking back and forwards a wee bit and making cryey noises. I haven't got any shoes or socks on and I don't want to step on any bits of splintery glass.

Mammy hasn't seen me.

I run quickly back downstairs and say to Daisy, Let's play in the back garden.

6

The veins underneath Mammy's eyes are all purple and broken where she's been crying so hard. Me and Daisy go round the house picking up her damp little balls of scrumpled-up loo roll. She wears sunglasses when we walk to the shops, and she doesn't take them off, even when we're inside. She doesn't make any noise when she cries, but the tears just keep dripping down her cheeks and off the end of her nose and chin, until she remembers to mop at them. She watches Children's BBC with us, and sometimes she sits on the floor beside us and watches us play Snap, but all the time she's crying.

—I'm sorry, girls, she says, and then she cries even more.

One evening, we bake fairy cakes, and her tears drip into the mixture, and then she starts crying so much that she has to go and lie down on the sofa, and she forgets to cook the fairy cakes. Me and Daisy don't mind. We eat them for tea just as they are, scooping them out of the paper cases with our fingers and licking our fingers afterwards. They taste nicer just mixture. There's enough left for breakfast the next morning. Mammy comes down and sees us sitting at the table sucking at the paper cases. Mammy's dressed and she's tied back her hair and put some lipstick on. Her face is puffy but she's stopped crying so maybe she's feeling better. Daisy and I stop eating and look at her.

—Mammy? Daisy goes.

—Jesus, girls! she goes. What are youse at?

—You forgot to cook them, Mammy, Daisy goes.

I jab Daisy with my elbow. But Mammy doesn't seem to have heard. She rinses a dishcloth in the sink and wipes the table and clears away the sticky fairy-cake cases.

Are there no more Shreddies? she goes, opening the cupboard.

There haven't been any Shreddies or milk for ages. We haven't been to the shops for days. But I don't say anything. It's been OK because there've been honey sandwiches and they taste nicer than Shreddies, even with sugar on top which we're only allowed for a treat.

Then Mammy goes, Right, get yourselves upstairs and let's get the two of youse washed and respectable-looking.

Mammy plaits our hair and buttons up the backs of our velvet dresses. It's too hot for our velvet dresses. And mine's too small for me.

—You've grown, Saoirse! Mammy says, crossly. Well, I don't have time to let out the seams. Breathe in! I want you looking presentable.

The buttons up the back of the dress feel like they're about to pop. Daisy is fidgeting with the lacy collar of her dress.

—It's itchy, Mammy, she goes, but Mammy ignores her. Then, Where are we going? Daisy asks.

—We're going to church, Mammy says, giving my dress a final yank.

To church? I look at Daisy and Daisy looks at me. We don't go to church, not even at Christmas, when everyone else goes to church. Daddy says that church is Magicking Nonsense, and Mammy taught us that whenever anyone asks what religion we are, we should answer, We don't go to church.

We take the same buses as if we're going to Isabella's, or the ice-cream parlour, except Isabella's left for Italy now and the ice-cream parlour is closed. Daisy's forgotten about that.

—Are we going to have an ice cream after? she goes.

—No we are not, I tell her, but she asks Mammy anyway.

—We'll see, Mammy says, but she says it in a voice that means she isn't really listening.

—I'm ho-ot, Daisy says.

I'm hot, too. The backs of my legs where the dress rides up are sticking to the seat. But I tell Daisy she's not hot and to shush.

The church is a big, grey, square building, with black bars across the outsides of the windows like a prison. Me and Daisy hold hands walking up the steps. Mammy walks on ahead, her high-heeled shoes clip-clopping on the stone. People are singing when we slip in through the heavy doors, and tiptoe to a bench right at the back.

—*A great sign appeared in heaven: a woman clothed with the sun, the moon beneath her feet, and a crown of twelve stars on her head.*

—Oh! Is it Étaín? Daisy whispers in my ear. Étaín is clothed in the gold of the sun and the silver of the moon.

—Is it? Sha-sha? Is it?

—Shh. Mammy said we're not to be talking.

Mammy closes her eyes and murmurs, Amen. Daisy reaches for my hand. Her hand is damp and sticky. Mammy's looking down at her shoes, but she still seems to know when the rest of the people are about to speak, and she speaks with them, exactly in time.

—Lord have mercy, the priest goes.

—Lord have mercy, Mammy says softly, with the rest of the people.

—Christ have mercy.

—Christ have mercy.

—Lord have mercy.

—Lord have mercy.

By the end, Mammy's only just managing to whisper the words.

Me and Daisy are too scared to be bored, and we don't fidget, not once. Don't you dare fidget, Mammy'd hissed at us as we were sitting down. The benches are slippery and our feet don't touch the floor and we can't see over the heads of the people in front of us but we don't shuffle about, or say a single word. But Mammy doesn't notice how good we've been. As everyone leaves, we stay sitting, and Mammy sits straight-backed, staring ahead, her hands folded in her lap. When the church is empty, Mammy gets up and goes to speak to the priest. They talk for a long time. Once, Mammy points over at me and Daisy, and the priest looks at us, and I can feel my face getting hot. I've got cramp in my leg but I sit as still as I can and hold Daisy's hand tight. When they turn away, me and Daisy slide down off the bench, and go quietly to the side of the church to look at the paintings and the statues and the candles. When the priest's finished talking to Mammy, he comes and kneels down beside us, and looks up at the big gloomy painting of Baby Jesus's mother holding Baby Jesus.

—You see that baby? he says, after a while. Do you know who he is?

—Baby Jesus, I whisper.

—Good girl, he says. That's right. And he grew up and saved the world.

—Why's his mammy so sad, then? Daisy asks, staring at Baby Jesus's mother's smooth, blank face.

—Perhaps, the priest goes, slowly, perhaps all mammies are sad that their wee babbies are going to grow up and they can't always protect them from the bad things that'll happen to them.

—Oh, says Daisy.

Then the priest goes, You're six years of age, are you, Saoirse?

—Six and three-quarters and soon I'll be seven.

—You'll soon be seven, will you? Ach, sure you're almost grown-up so you are!

—I'm four, goes Daisy.

—Are you indeed? he goes. Then he goes, Do you girls say your prayers?

Daisy shakes her head, suddenly shy.

—*Now-I-lay-me-down-to-sleep-I-pray-the-Lord-my-soul-to-keep*, I gabble. It's the one they learn us at school.

He smiles.

—I've got something for youse, then.

He gives us each a piece of stiff card, with swirly gold lettering and drawings of curly-haired children and lambs. *A Child's Bedtime Prayer*, it says along the top.

—Your mammy'll help you to read it, he says.

The priest clasps Mammy's hands for a long time.

—You've done the right thing, he goes.

—Thank you, Father, she goes.

—Sha-sha? goes Daisy, tugging at my sleeve. He's not Mammy's daddy!

—Shh, I go.

—The Church is always here for its children, he says.

I poke Daisy. I think he means us. Daisy is staring up at the gold carvings hanging from the edges of the ceiling. I try and look Respectable and Presentable in my velvet dress that's too hot and tight for me.

—Remember the Memorare, the priest says.

—*Remember O most loving Virgin Mary that it is a thing unheard of that anyone ever had recourse to your protection implored your help or sought your intercession and was left forsaken*, Mammy goes, all in one breath, and she sounds like Daisy saying the alphabet.

—Yes, he says. It will bring you great comfort.

Mammy doesn't say anything. Her face is pale in the shadows. She stares up at him for a long time before turning away. Then, Come on, girls, she goes.

She turns and walks quickly out of the church, her shoes making a loud noise on the silent stone floors. Me and Daisy hurry behind her, clutching each other's hands.

7

Mammy has put all of Daddy's clothes and shoes and tapes and things in boxes in the hallway. She made me sit beside her and hold the end of the masking tape for her while she taped the boxes up. We have to squeeze past the boxes to get up the stairs.

—What's going to happen? Daisy keeps asking me, over and over again. But I don't know, and I don't want to ask Mammy.

Me and Daisy are playing on the swing when we hear the sound of a car in the drive. It sounds like Daddy's Astra. We look at each other, and I let go of the ropes where I'm pushing Daisy and run round the side of the house.

—Wait for me! Daisy screams. Wait for me!

Daddy hugs us both for a long time. He smells the same as always and he bristles my cheek like he always does.

—Mammy, Mammy! Daisy shrieks, dancing inside. Daddy's back!

Mammy is sitting at the kitchen table reading a letter. She folds it up and puts it in her pocket and looks at Daddy when he comes in, but she doesn't say anything. Daddy clears his throat.

—Shall we unpack Daddy's things? Daisy asks.

Daddy makes a noise that isn't words. He came in the back door with us and he hasn't seen the boxes in the hall yet. Mammy looks at Daddy. She clears her throat. Then she looks away.

—Girls, go back outside and play for a wee bit, Daddy says. We don't move.

—Girls, Daddy says, in the same quiet voice.

Mammy and Daddy stay inside for a long time. Me and Daisy are hungry. But we don't want to go back in. I tell Daisy to creep up to the kitchen window and try and listen in. But she won't, and I won't, either.

Daddy comes to the back door.

—Come on, Sunshine, come on, Daisy! he calls. I'm taking you to the zoo!

—The zoo? I say.

—Aren't you excited? Daddy says.

We eat biscuits and crisps and apples in the car: me, Daisy and Daddy; Mammy isn't coming with us.

—Will there be elephants? Daisy goes.

—I should think so, Daddy goes. And snakes. And penguins, and . . . let's see, and – tigers!

—Tigers!

Daddy makes a tiger noise and Daisy squeals and hides her face in her hands.

—I think Emily might be scared of tigers, Daisy goes, after a bit. She hugs Emily tight.

—Daisy, goes Daddy, you tell Emily that so long as I'm around not one of those mean auld tigers will hurt her. You tell her that!

—It's OK, Emily, Daisy says, straightening out Emily's plaits. Don't be a scaredy-cat. Everything will be OK, you hear me?

There is a long queue when we get to the zoo. When we get to the front, the lady behind the counter says that if we hurry, we might just be in time to see Feeding Time at the Penguin Enclosure.

—Feeding Time at the Penguin Enclosure? goes Daddy. Magic! How's about that, you two?

The lady hands us a map and Daddy looks at it for a second, then he grabs Daisy's hand – Let's a-go! – and we set off. We run past lots of the other animals' cages, but by the time we get to the Penguin Enclosure, the keepers, with their dark blue overalls and their big smelly buckets, are leaving. Daddy goes up to one of them.

—Is there any chance of throwing one more wee fish for the penguins? I've brought my wee girls here specially to see the penguins.

—Sorry, sir, goes the keeper. Feeding time's over, so it is.

—Aye, I can see that, but just one more wee fish?

—I'm sorry but, as I say, feeding time's over.

—What an ignorant man, Daddy goes, as the keeper walks away. You'd think he could find one more wee fish to throw, ey? Lazy bloody bastard.

—Daddy, goes Daisy when Daddy says that.

—What? Sorry, love. I'm sorry.

We watch the penguins and the seals for a bit. Daddy lifts Daisy on to his shoulders so she can see over the concrete barrier. Daisy clutches Emily tight so that Emily doesn't fall in. The Penguin Enclosure is bright blue, with rocks and pretend icebergs and wee waterfalls. The penguins are just standing about on the rocks not doing very much. There's a baby seal quite near us, and it watches us with big bright eyes.

—Oh, can I've a seal, Daddy? Daisy shouts when she sees it. Please? A wee babby seal?

—Where would you keep it? Daddy goes.

Daisy thinks.

—In the bath! It could go in the bath, oh please, Daddy!

—Will it eat up your fish pie for you? Daddy goes, in a serious voice.

—Yes! Daisy cries. Please, Daddy?

—Ach, come on, Daisy, Daddy goes. You can't have a seal for a pet. Let's go and see some other animals, shall we?

We see the monkeys in the Monkey House and we see a camel and we see a wee baby zebra hiding behind its mammy zebra. But Daisy still wants a seal. In the end, Daddy gets fed up and we walk all the way back to the shop by the entrance to buy Daisy a toy seal. Daddy buys me a book of animal stories.

—What shall we get Mammy? Daisy says.

—I don't think your mammy'll be wanting anything, Daddy says.

—She will, Daisy insists. A T-shirt! Or, or a pencil and rubber!

—I don't think so, love, goes Daddy.

But in the end, when we're at the till, he picks up a big box of chocolates.

—We'll give these to Mammy, all right?

There is an announcement that the zoo will be closing in half an hour. We haven't seen the tigers or the elephants yet, Daddy remembers. He looks at the map. The tigers and the elephants are at opposite ends of the zoo. We only have time to see one of them, he says.

—Tigers! Daisy says.

Daddy looks at me.

—Let Sunshine choose, he says.

I shrug. Daddy looks sad.

—OK then, tigers, I say. I'd like to see the tigers, I say again.

There are two tigers, and they have a big cage with a stream running through, and tyres hanging from ropes, and pretend caves.

—That's nice, isn't it, says Daddy, squeezing my shoulders. Lots of room for them to run around in, ey?

But both tigers are lying down in one of the concrete caves, and you can't see them properly.

—I'm sorry, girls, Daddy goes. I'm really sorry.

—It doesn't matter, Daddy, I go.

From the car park, you can see where the giant lies sleeping, buried under Cave Hill. You can make out the shape of him, his head and shoulders, and his massive lumpy body. Even on the sunniest of days, Cave Hill is dark and gloomy.

—What will happen when the giant wakes up? I ask.

But Daddy doesn't know.

—Perhaps he'll never wake up, Daddy suggests, after a bit. Then he adds, That giant has been asleep for hundreds of years without so much as stirring. Perhaps he's content to sleep on.

Daisy and I go to get into the car, but Daddy says he needs to Talk To Us. We sit at a wooden picnic table covered in crumbs and sticky smears. The bin nearby is overflowing and there is a spilt can of Coke on the ground right beside us and wasps are crawling around going in and out. I watch the wasps waving their little pointy bodies in the air.

—Sunshine, look at me, Daddy goes. Daddy and Mammy have been having a wee bit of trouble lately, he goes.

Then he pauses, and looks away. I look back down at the wasps.

—Is that why Mammy's always crying? Daisy says.

Mammy's always crying these days. Even if you try to hug her or draw her a drawing to cheer her up she still cries.

—Aye, it is, Daddy goes, slowly. He clears his throat, then he clears it again. Your mammy and I were young when we met. Your mammy was very young indeed. We thought we could be happy together. But, and you girls will understand this when you're older, sometimes, sometimes there're things that you can't change, or things that are too much for one person, or even for two people. Are you with me? Girls? Do you understand what I'm saying?

Me and Daisy are puzzled.

—Daddy loves you, you know that? You know that, Sunshine? Do you know that, Daisy?

—I love you too, Daddy, I falter.

—Daddy and Mammy can't live together any more, Daddy goes. So Daddy's going to move out. I'll still see you, as much as possible, and it doesn't mean I don't love you, or I love you any less, d'ye hear me?

—But where are you going to live, Daddy? Daisy bleats.

Daddy doesn't say anything.

—Are you going to have a new family, Daddy? Daisy whispers in a tiny voice.

Daddy turns away. His shoulders are shuddering.

—Your mammy and I tried. I swear to God we did! But it wasn't enough.

—Daddy, you've made Emily cry, goes Daisy.

—I'm sorry, wee love, goes Daddy, and he bends down and kisses Daisy's forehead.

—I want to go home now, I say.

—Me too, says Daisy.

Daisy is falling asleep when we get in. Daddy puts us to bed, and then he sits at the edge of my bed and strokes my hair. He says that there is a chance that he is going to be Posted

Elsewhere by his job, and it might be for a long time. I start to laugh and laugh and laugh at the idea of Daddy all bundled up with paper and sellotape and stamps on his forehead being shoved into a postbox. I laugh so hard I can't breathe but I can't stop laughing. Daddy scoops me up and presses me against his chest and suddenly I feel floppy like a rag doll.

—Look after your mammy and your sister for me, won't you? he goes.

I want to say, Please don't go, Daddy. But my throat has closed over and no words will come out.

The next day, Daddy's boxes are gone from the hallway.

8

Daisy keeps pestering Mammy, asking why Daddy's gone away again and when he'll be coming back and Mammy starts to sob. Then she locks herself in her bedroom and we hear the sound of a bottle smashing, and Daisy is scared, so we run outside to play Tiger Tamers in the back garden. Ever since the zoo, Tiger Tamers is our new best game. One person has to be a Wild Tiger and the other person has to be a Tamer and the Tamer has to catch the Wild Tiger. I say I'll be the Tamer and Daisy can be the Wild Tiger, even though she isn't a very good Wild Tiger because she's always far too easy to Catch and Tame.

We play for a bit. Then all of a sudden it starts to thunder and rain. The sky goes dark and thunder crashes across the sky and before we can get inside there's rain pouring down like out of buckets and we're soaked to the skin.

There's nothing to do inside and Daisy keeps sniffling and whingeing that she's cold and her sore ear is sore. I creep upstairs and pull the duvet off my bed and drag it downstairs and make a nest for us in the living room, and we sit there for a bit. I find one of my Peter-and-Jane books that I'm practising reading for when school starts again. I've been trying to teach Daisy how to read, but Daisy says reading is boring. All that ever happens in my school books is Peter-and-Jane Play in the Garden with their Dog, or Peter-and-Jane Go to the Supermarket with their Mother. Daisy likes it better when we make up our own stories, like Peter-and-Jane Fight the Dragons, or Peter-and-Jane Go to the Enchanted Castle of Faery. But I'm bored of Peter-and-Jane. It's too early for Children's BBC.

—I'm hungry, goes Daisy. I want a honey sandwich.

We go into the kitchen. But there's no more bread for sandwiches. We go back to our nest in the living room.

The box of zoo chocolates that Daddy bought for Mammy is on the coffee table. It's made of glittering golden cardboard, and it's wrapped with frothy tissue paper, and tied with red-and-gold ribbons. I make Daisy untie one of the bows. She tears some of the tissue paper by mistake, and looks up at me, scared. I get scared, too, and I try and retie the bow, but the tissue paper tears some more and the bow comes off, and the box is open.

—Dare you to eat one, I go.

—No, Daisy goes.

—Dare you.

—You first.

So I eat a chocolate, and make Daisy eat one, too. Then I eat another one, and so does Daisy, and then I eat two at a time, and I make Daisy open her mouth for more even when she hasn't finished swallowing. Soon our fingers and mouths are sticky with chocolate and caramel and strawberry fondant and we eat and eat until we've eaten the whole box.

—I feel sick, Daisy goes.

I feel sick as well. Then Daisy bokes up all over the duvet and all over the carpet, a smelly mess of chocolate-coloured puke, lumpy with bits of peanut. Daisy gurns at the top of her voice and Mammy comes stumbling down the stairs, and when she sees the state of the room, and the chocolate dribbling down our chins, and the pile of ripped tissue paper and cardboard, she explodes with anger. She grabs Daisy by the arm and drags her into the kitchen, and scrubs at her mouth with the dishcloth. Then she slaps me across the face and screams that both of us are to go to bed, right now.

Later on, I tiptoe downstairs to say sorry, but Mammy is curled up in the sofa in the living room crying. She isn't making any noise but she's crying so hard her whole body is trembling and her face is all twisted up. I cuddle in beside her, and say we're sorry we ate the chocolates, but she doesn't say anything; she just hugs me tight and shakes with crying. Daisy followed me down the stairs, but she was afraid of Mammy seeing her out of bed, so she sat on the bottom stair for a bit until she must've got bored and I hear the door go, so she must've gone outside, managing the snib all by herself. The rain has stopped, but the back garden is all wet and muddy, so Daisy plays in the driveway at the front of the house. I can see her through the living-room window, and she waves at me, and she jumps about like she's a Wild Tiger. You need two people to play Tiger Tamers properly. But Mammy's stopped shaking, and she's got her eyes closed like she's sleeping, and she's holding me tight, and I don't want to leave her, so I stay snuggled up with her on the sofa. Daisy swings on the front gate for a while, but she's too small to make it swing properly. So then she picks up our yellow bouncy ball and tries to balance it on her nose like the seal in my animal book from the zoo. But the ball keeps falling off and bouncing away. Then it bounces right out of the gate and into the road. Daisy runs after it and I can't see her any more.

*

65

A car horn blasts suddenly and it goes on and on the noise of it tearing through the air and on top of the car horn a shrieking noise a bang then: there is nothing.

Since they blocked off the main road with the Army barricades, cars have been using our road as a short cut. It's disgraceful, Mammy says, and she says someone should do something about it because they drive too fast: racing to beat the lights at the big traffic lights. Just a few days ago a wee lad from up the top of the street escaped getting knocked down by a short-cutter by no more than the skin of his teeth.

I wriggle out of Mammy's arms and run to open the front door.

—Daisy! I shout.

There is no answer. I shout again, at the top of my voice. Then I think, maybe it's just that Daisy can't hear because of her gluey ear.

Mammy has woken up.

—What was that? she calls, thickly. That sounded like it was just outside our house.

I start to run down the drive, and I haven't got any shoes or socks on and the gravel is cutting my feet. Behind me, I hear Mammy running, too.

—Jesus Christ, Saoirse, where's your sister? she shouts.

The Weather Has Broken, is what the grown-ups say. Lightning rips through the high blue sky, and the rain comes pouring through the cracks, pouring and pouring, as if it'll never stop.

*

I decide that I'll use my birthday wish to wish Daisy better. But on the day that I turn seven, nobody remembers that it's my birthday. There's no cards, no presents, no nothing; and no cake and candles to wish on.

9

Daddy has come back and he's been sleeping on the living-room sofa, and he and Mammy take it in turns to go to the hospital to visit Daisy so there's always someone with her.

—Can I go? I ask, every day. Why don't I get to go and see Daisy?

But Daddy says children aren't allowed at the hospital. One day, Mammy and Daddy both have to go to the hospital, and so I have to stay with the girl across the road. I don't like the girl across the road. Jennifer, you call her. She was one of the ones who put dog turd mud on our doorstep. Jennifer's a year older than I am and she's big and fat with little piggy eyes. She always wears her hair in a ponytail with three scrunchies.

We're sitting in her bedroom because her mammy told her to take me up and show me her bedroom. She's got posters of the Glentoran football team on the wall.

—I bet you've never been to a Glens match, she goes.

I don't say anything.

—I bet you've never, she goes again, all sly.

I look out of her window at my house across the road. It's raining, and the two fir trees guarding the house look all sad and droopy. Jennifer comes up behind me. She's holding a can of Impulse Body Spray. She sprays it at me.

—You stink, she says. Did you know that?

—Sticks-and-stones-will-break-my-bones-but-names-will-never-hurt-me, I chant at her.

—You're a stinking Taig, she says. Yer ma's a Taig.

68

Then she pinches my arm. I hit her back, right in the middle of her fat piggy face, as hard as I can. She starts gurning and goes running off to tell her mammy on me. Her mammy marches up the stairs and takes me by the arm and trails me down to sit at the kitchen table with my arms folded. Then I hear Jennifer's mammy saying to Jennifer in the hall, And as for you, you should be feeling sorry for her, not fighting with her, d'ye hear me?

Daddy doesn't pick me up until late that night. But I don't eat a single bite of the burger and chips that the woman gives me for tea.

—I'm never going to Jennifer's again, I say to Daddy. Ever.

—Sunshine, he goes.

—You can't make me, I go. I'll run away if you make me.

—Please, love, he goes. Daddy's face is all grey and his eyes are yellow.

—I'm big enough to look after myself, I go. I am. I can look after myself.

—WILL YOU BE QUIET! Daddy gulders, suddenly, right in my face. For crying out loud!

I pull my hand out of his.

—I hate you! I go.

When we get in, Daddy says, Get yourself to bed.

—I'm hungry, I say.

—I said, go to bed!

—But I'm hungry!

I didn't even eat one weeny bite of Jennifer's mammy's burger and chips. And now it's way past teatime and my tummy's growling.

—I'm not going to bed, I say.

Daddy lunges at me and picks me up and carries me up

the stairs. He throws me down on to the bed. I'm kicking and screaming.

—I hate you! I shout. I hate you!

Daddy wakes me up in the middle of the night.

—Get dressed as quick as you can, he goes. We're going to the hospital right away.

My fingers are sleepy and the T-bars of my sandals won't do up. Daddy picks me up and carries me from the porch to the Astra, and he straps me in the front seat. I've never been in the front of the car before, and Daddy doesn't even bother with my booster seat.

It feels like me and Daddy are the only ones up in the whole of the world. But I don't say anything because I'm not speaking to Daddy.

The early morning sky is thick and grey when we get to the hospital. As Daddy parks the car, it skids through the puddles left over from yesterday's rain, and when we get out, the water goes over the top of my sandals and soaks through my socks. Daddy is walking fast and I have to hop and skip and splash to keep up with him. There is a row of trees by the entrance, their trunks all black and slimy, with yellow mushrooms growing from their roots. Daddy sits me in a seat by the entrance, and there is a whoosh of damp, mouldy-smelling air every time the doors slide open. I zip my anorak right up to the neck, and pull the hood down over my head. People walk muddy footprints across the pale green floor. Daddy doesn't come back. But a nurse who smells of peppermint takes me to a room with lots of toys and colouring-in books. She gives me a picture of a snowman, and once I've coloured his scarf and carrot-nose and eyes the nurse tells me to colour in his body, but you don't colour snowmen in, and anyway, all of the good crayons are broken. On the back of the snowman picture, I draw a tiger being tamed.

The Peppermint Nurse and I are playing with some Lego, except she's no good because she doesn't know what a Fairy Castle should look like and she keeps on trying to make it look like a normal house. Then Daddy comes to the door, and he doesn't come in, he just stands there. I'm sorry I said I hated him.

—Look, Daddy! I say, and I hold up the picture of my tiger that I drew. But he doesn't say anything, and all of a sudden I am scared. He stares at me but he doesn't even look at my tiger. He kneels down, only he kind of crumples, knocking over the Lego castle, and he says in a quiet voice that Daisy has gone on a Journey and won't be coming back. Then the nurse bends over and hugs me too tightly and I can't breathe and her disinfectanty pepperminty smell is suffocating me.

I pull away and ask her where Daisy has gone, and she says, To a Magical Kingdom in the Sky.

—Like Tir-nan-Og? I say. She looks at me.

—Yes, she says, slowly. Like Tir-nan-Og.

—Will she be able to get back? I say.

—No, love, the nurse says. She's fallen asleep, see; a long, long sleep.

Like the wasting Sickness of Cúchulainn.

And then I know: just like Emer got her enchanted potion and the spell to rescue Cúchulainn from the land of the *Síde*, I have to find a way to bring back Daisy before it's too late.

IO

We sleep together in Mammy-and-Daddy's bed, Mammy and me. During the night, she cuddles me, but during the day, she won't talk to me, and some days she won't even look at me.

—Don't worry, Mammy, I whisper. Daisy will be back.

Mammy grabs my shoulders and shakes me and shakes me and shakes me.

—*Saoirse!* Holy God, Saoirse! Your wee sister'll not be back! Why can you not understand me? Why will you not understand? Jesus help me! Daisy's – Daisy's—

But Mammy can't hardly say Daisy's name, and she pushes me away.

I wake up sweating, tangled up in the sheets.

What have you done? How could you? Get away from me, go on, get away, I can't bear to touch you. Get away from me I said! What have you done, what have you done?

Dusty dust, the man says, in a deep and sad voice. Dusty dust.

Nobody knows that Daisy's just sleeping an enchanted sleep. If we don't bring her back from Tir-nan-Og, from the enchanted castle of the *Síde*, if we don't bring her back soon, then she will turn to dust, for people of our world cannot live in the land of Faery for long. But there's nobody to help me. I keep on trying to explain to Mammy and Daddy but it's no use because they don't listen. Nobody will listen. Daisy will suffocate under the earth. I scream.

II

Daisy is gone, and Daddy is gone, and although Mammy doesn't tell me so, I know I'm not to speak to her of either of them any more. So now it's just me and Mammy, and me and Mammy are leaving the house, and Belfast, For Ever.

She tells me to play in the garden while she finishes packing the suitcases and sorting out what we'll take with us and what all's to go down to the charity shop. I climb into the biggest fir tree. It's been raining, and the bark is black and slimy. It smears greeny-brown streaks down my dungarees. Mammy will be cross, I think. Then I think that she might not notice. She didn't notice that she buttoned my cardigan over my pyjama top this morning.

I squash Emily in between the trunk and a branch, where she won't fall out. Through the branches, I can see down the street as far as Wee Man's house. His house has a flag hanging from each of the upstairs windows: a big Union flag and a Red Hand of Ulster. The gate of his house is painted red, white and blue to match the red, white and blue kerbs and the red, white and blue bunting that's strung up between the lampposts. Wee Man's brother organized the painting of the kerbs and the stringing of the bunting at the beginning of the summer, and me and Daisy watched from up in the fir tree, the other fir tree, the smaller one, because it's easier to climb and Daisy wasn't as good at climbing as me. We were the only ones not allowed to do the painting, and that's when Jennifer across the road started swinging on our gate and shouting that our eyes were too close together.

The street's empty, because everyone else has to go to school. This is the first year I am big enough to have lunch in the canteen, and stay for afternoon school, and wear a tie. Daddy taught me how to knot a tie. I practised until I could do it by myself. Mammy doesn't know if the new uniform, in the new school I'll be going to, will have a tie. When I ask her, she says, And how do you think I know, or she says, Away off and play and don't be plaguing me.

I stay in the tree until Mammy comes out and calls for me to run down the chippy to get cod and chips for tea.

—Can I have sausage instead?

—If you like, she shrugs.

—Can I have two sausages? In batter?

—If that's what you want, she goes.

We eat straight from the newspaper. I feel sick halfway through the first sausage, when I find a lump of gristle. I push the soft, warm, greasy package away from me to the other side of the table. Mammy doesn't eat hers, either.

There's a tape cassette of Mammy and Daddy singing songs with me and Daisy. On one side, Daddy sings 'Froggy Went Ah-Kortin' and 'Daisy, Daisy' and Mammy sings some of her Cúchulainn songs and on the second side there's me singing the whole of 'Molly Malone', doing a cackly voice for the final verse where it's her ghost pushing the barrow through streets broad and narrow. On the tape, Mammy and Daddy applaud at the end of me singing and then I start the song all over again and they laugh. Then Daddy sings the beginning of 'O Soldier, Soldier, Won't You Marry Me, With Your Musket, Fife and Drum' and Mammy-on-the-tape gets cross and stops the recording so the tape cuts out.

Mammy sits at the kitchen table with piles of things that aren't packed yet all around her, and she plays the tape over and over. Jennifer and Jennifer's mammy call in to say goodbye. Mammy makes a pot of tea for her and Jennifer's mammy and she finds orange squash and pink wafer biscuits for me and Jennifer. Piggy Jennifer takes two pink wafer biscuits at once and stuffs them into her mouth and then starts coughing and choking because they're so dusty. I stick out my tongue at her and she glares at me.

They run out of things to say before the juice or the tea is even halfway drunk.

—I found a tape cassette, says Mammy.

—Oh? says the woman.

Please, Mammy, I think as hard as I can. Please no.

—Would you like to hear it? says Mammy.

I see Jennifer give a quick sideways look at her mammy.

Mammy presses *play*, and Daddy starts to sing 'Daisy, Daisy'.

Jennifer smirks at her mammy. Her mammy frowns at her. Then Mammy covers her face with her hands and she's making funny low noises with an open, gulping mouth.

I know fat Jennifer with her big bloated face will be saving it all up to tell to Baps and Wee Man and the others on our street.

Mammy starts saying she's sorry. The woman pats Mammy's arm and Jennifer grins a slow, mean grin at me.

They leave without finishing their tea and juice. While Mammy's closing the door behind them, I cut the spool and pretend that the tape player mangled it.

On the morning of the day we're leaving, I wake up early because the house is empty now and it feels like it's wanting to be alone. The tables and chairs and sofa went a couple of days ago, loaded up higgledy-piggledy in a lorry, and only the beds and a few odd bits and pieces of furniture are left. The new people that'll be living in our house are bringing their own curtains and carpets, so our curtains have been taken down and our carpets have been ripped up. The raw floorboards creak when you step on them and they keep spiking our feet with splinters; they don't like people walking over them. Mammy says we're leaving because the house is too full of memories. But I think the memories were soaked into the sofas, and the toys, and into the big wooden table in the kitchen, and the rug in the hall we used to play Flying Carpets on. There's nothing between the bare walls and floors now, just me and Mammy too loud in the echoey place.

I put on my jeans and my red woolly jumper with all the sheep jumping over fences. Then I buckle my T-bar sandals and zip up my bright pink anorak with the hood. My crayons and my favourite books and my ballerina box are packed in my school satchel, so I sit quietly holding Emily until Mammy wakes up.

Mammy plaits my hair in two plaits like she sometimes did for school. She pulls my hair too tight but I don't say anything, and when she's finished I tug at the bits of hair at the nape of my neck until they come loose. Then we sit on the stairs waiting for the taxi to come. There's no cereal left, or bread for toast, but Mammy makes some tea and for me she makes Cambric Tea. Cambric Tea is special tea for little girls who aren't old enough for proper grown-up tea. It's made from hot water and milk, with one squeeze of a teabag – dipped inandout – quick as that. It burns my mouth at first, and by the time it cools down there is a thin rubbery skin over the surface. Normally, finding skin on my bedtime cocoa makes me feel sick and I make Mammy take it away with a spoon, but I don't want her to think that I don't want the Cambric Tea that she made for me so I make sure she isn't looking and then I poke at the slimy skin with one finger and wipe it on the banister. When we've finished, Mammy takes the mugs into the kitchen and she washes them up. She goes to the drawer for a teatowel, then she stops, and she stands for a second, looking at the mugs. Then she shrugs and sets them upside down on the draining board, and she unplugs the kettle and coils the flex round the base, and stores it neatly in a cupboard, and then the taxi comes to take us to the bus station. The taxi man and Mammy carry our suitcases out, and I help by dragging them down the porch steps until Mammy tells me to get into the car because I'm getting wet. It's drizzling, but my anorak is done up right to the neck and I've put the hood up so I'm not wet at all. I tell Mammy this, and not to worry, and she snaps at me that I'm in the way and would I just do as she says and get into the car. I don't want to because I haven't yet said goodbye to the fir trees that used to guard the house.

—Saoirse! You are to get into that taxi this instant and you are to sit quietly while I lock up and run across the road with the keys, understand!

—I don't want to.

—You'll do as I tell you, she says, and she smacks the back of my legs.

—You hit me!

—Aye, and you'd better be in that car by the count of three or else I'll give you a proper hiding. One!

—Daddy would never smack me! I scream at her.

—Two!

—Daddy wouldn't shout at me like that!

—Well, your daddy'll not be back to smack you or

otherwise. He's gone for good. For ever. D'ye hear me? Now, don't make me count to three.

Daddy's gone for good. He'll not be back. For ever.

—Mammy! It suddenly occurs to me. But if he does come back, how will Daddy know where to find us?

But Mammy doesn't answer.

—Three! she roars, and she jerks at the sleeve of my anorak and shoves me into the back seat of the taxi, then slams the door. So I don't get to say goodbye or to tell the fir trees that it wasn't their fault. I always told Daisy the fir trees were magic guardians who'd watch over us. But it wasn't their fault.

Mammy's hardly spoken a word to me since we left the house. The whole coach journey she sits with her head back on the headrest and her eyes closed and her hands slack in her lap, but I know she isn't sleeping. She sits like that even when the coach driver shouts that we've arrived in Stroke City, and all the other people get off. I have to pat her cheeks and say, Mammy, Mammy, we're here, Mammy, before she opens her eyes and when she opens them they're all starey, like they aren't seeing anything. Our suitcases are dumped in a pile on the tarmac, and it's beginning to spit with rain. I pull up my hood, but Mammy doesn't even bother to do up her mac, like she hasn't even noticed the drizzle. I spell out the writing painted under murals on the walls opposite. 'FREE DERRY'. 'BRITISH OUT'. 'INLA'.

—What's Inn-lah? I say, but Mammy doesn't hear me.

We stand there for a few minutes, and a thin white mist settles over Mammy's hair and face and shoulders.

—D'ye need a hand with them bags? a voice goes. I look up. It's an old man who was sitting just across from us on the coach.

—Oh . . . Mammy turns, vague. We're waiting for someone.

The man nods up at the sky.

—Aye, but it's getting heavier, so it is. You'd mebbe be best off waiting inside somewhere. I seen you get off the coach with all them bags. Here, it's no bother.

He picks up two of the suitcases, and Mammy picks up the wheely suitcase and the holdall. I pick up my gym bag and my satchel. We walk across the street and along a bit to a coffee shop. The man shoulders the door open and shepherds us inside, and a warm, stale, greasy fug surrounds us. A bell tinkles as the door closes behind us. We set the bags and cases down.

—There you go, the old man says.

He seems nice. I think, maybe if we're friendly to him he'll stay and pretend to be my grandpa for a bit, if he's nowhere else to go. He doesn't look like he's in a hurry to go anywhere. He stands smiling at me and Mammy. Mammy's staring straight in front of her. I smile back at the man, a little smile, and he smiles a big smile at me.

—There you go, the man says again. Then he goes, Well. Ach well. Miserable day for youse. Miserable day an' all.

Mammy blinks, and notices him still standing there.

—Thank you, she goes, nodding at our bags.

—No problem, the old man says, and he winks at me. You off for a wee holiday, are ye? Have yourself a good trip now.

He hunches his shoulders up into his coat and leaves the coffee shop, clattering the glass door shut behind him. Mammy crumples into a chair, and I sit opposite her. A girl calls over from behind the counter.

—What are youse havin'?

—Are you hungry? Mammy asks me.

I shake my head.

—You'd better have something to eat. We may not get there until late.

I get a sausage, egg and chips with a glass of Club Orange, and Mammy gets a pot of tea. She adds three spoonfuls of sugar from the metal pot, and stirs it slowly. Then, without drinking it, she gets up.

—Sit you here and mind the bags, she goes. I've a phone call to make.

She asks the girl behind the counter for the use of a phone, and the girl says the phone's not for customer use but there's a payphone just across the road. I shift my chair round so I can see Mammy through the door of the coffee shop. The glass walls of the phone box have been smashed in and she's all hunched up against the rain and the cold. I cut my sausage up into little bits to make sure there's no gristle, and I wipe the runny egg yolk up. But I'm not hungry. I suck my Club Orange through the straw, then blow it back down in bubbles. I'm not thirsty either. Mammy finishes her phone call and comes back in, drenched, her hair sticking to her face in long straggly strands.

—Brendan's on his way, she says. He'll be here before too long.

We are going to live with my brand new aunt and uncle, Mammy's big sister Aunty Bernadette and her husband Uncle Brendan. I've never had an aunt and uncle before. Only Grandpa Tony and he wasn't even a real grandpa; we only called him that. When Mammy told me, when we'd started packing up the house and the removals men were arriving to take the furniture away, I asked, Will there be any cousins there? Will I have new cousins to play with?

—No, Mammy said, and she added emphatically, And you're not to go plaguing the life out of your aunt and uncle, you hear me? You're to be quiet and well-behaved and do as you're told. They're not used to children so you mustn't make a nuisance of yourself.

Mammy closes her eyes. Little drips of water are trickling down her face and off the end of her nose and she doesn't wipe them away. I pick up a shiny paper napkin and dry her face for her.

—Jesus, she says, softly; then again, Jesus.

With the bubbles from the fizzy orange all sharp and sticky up the back of my nose, my tummy starts to feel sore.

Can we go back, Mammy? is what I want to say, but I don't say it, because I know that we can't; I know that we've gone too far now.

PART TWO
Gweebarra Bay

12

There's a dead seal washed up on the strand. I can see it from my window. It's lying just beyond the low-water mark, and it's all tangled up in seaweed. For a moment, I think: Holy God, it's a person, and I push open the skylight and lean out as far as I can to get a better look.

There was a storm last night. A powerful fierce storm, in the early hours of the morning. There were big waves crashing down on the beach all night, and what with the noise of it, the roaring of the waves and the howling of the wind, I couldn't sleep properly. Any time I did start to drift off I had the weirdest dreams, and I kept waking up with a jerk, the sweat running off me, convinced I could hear screaming.

Maybe it's a fisherman off one of the lobster boats, I think when I see the body on the sand. Maybe the fishermen went out, and then the storm blew up suddenly, and the boat couldn't make it back into the harbour at Portnoo. Looking closely, you can see it's not the right shape to be a person, but I run down to the shore anyway. I'm still in my pyjamas, and I've not got any shoes on, and the beach is cold and slimy with seaweed. The seal is lying on its back, all plump and round and blotchy grey. I poke it with a bit of driftwood to make sure it's not alive, and the feel of it makes me want to boke. It's like damp bread or something. Doughy. Kind of spongy. I use the driftwood to scrape the seaweed from round its head, and I see a big black eye, shiny and swollen. I drop the stick and take a step back from it but I can't stop looking at it. Christ, it's boggin'.

—What are you at footerin' about out there for? Aunt Bernadette shouts from the back porch. And dressed in next to nothing at all! Saoirse, for the love of God you'll catch your death. Come on in and get your breakfast in you, you'll be late for school!

I turn and run back up to the house, like a spell's been broken. But seeing a dead seal is unlucky, and I can't quite shake off the creeping feeling that something bad's on its way.

It's chilly for June. We're having unseasonably bad weather for this time of year, everyone agrees, and my aunt and uncle are worried because bookings for the summer are already down on last year, and we didn't have a particularly good Easter. And the hack of that storm last night, and it nearly summer! they say. You just shouldn't get storms like that at this time of year. When I get home from school, I walk down to the edge of the strand. High tide's been and gone, and the beach is smooth, clear of the seaweed and driftwood and debris of the storm, and the seal is gone, too. The wind is up, and blowing in gusty snatches. I stand for a bit, watching the waves shatter into froth and foam on the jagged outcrop of rocks just beyond the headland, then I shiver suddenly, and go back to the house.

Inside, the kitchen is warm and stuffy, and condensation is running down the windows in tiny rivulets. My aunty's busy baking soda bread. She's stooped over the range, her sleeves rolled up and her big mottled arms like slabs of meat. I watch her back for a bit. She doesn't say anything, and nor do I. When she eventually turns round, it's to say, Pass us the buttermilk out of the pantry, will you?

I lift the heavy blue jug with both hands and bring it in to the kitchen table without a word.

—How was school? she says.

—Grand.

—Did you get your tests back?

—Aye.

—And?

—Yeah. I got second in Irish.

—Your uncle'll be proud of you.

—Where is he?

—He's taken himself down to Sheehy's for a quick pint. She pauses, hands on her hips. Give us a hand, will you, love?

—You feeding the five thousand or something or is it Farmer Dennehy coming over for his tea?

—Your cousin Michael and his Brid are coming over with the baby.

Michael Deegan's not my cousin. He's Uncle Brendan's cousin, but he's only a few years older than me, and my uncle has always regarded him as a sort-of son.

—Well, are you going to stand there with your two arms the same length or will you give us a hand? she goes.

Baking bread was one of the first things my aunty taught me when I came to live at Gweebarra Sands. In a busy summer, Aunt Bernadette will bake three or maybe four batches of sodas a day; tourists just can't get enough of it. I used to stand on a wee stool to reach up to the counter, and knead my own dough in a little plastic basin. Once, I made soda bread for my father when he was coming up to visit. In Belfast, on Saturday mornings, my father would go down the Ormeau Road to the bakery to buy sodie farls. There's nothing sets you up like a negg soda, he'd say. Mammy'd fry the sodie bread on both sides so as it was crisp, but not burnt, and she'd slip a sunny-side-up egg on top of it. Daisy and I ate the spongy bread buttered with strawberry jam. Some days it was still warm when Daddy brought it home, and when Mammy cut it open, steam would puff out of it. I baked soda bread for my father, once, thinking it would make him happy. But he just went all quiet when I proudly handed him the paper bag.

I finish scoring the surface of the dough and slide it into the oven. I don't like it when I remember things, like soda bread and the bakery on the Ormeau Road and Belfast.

—There, I go, slamming the Aga door.

—Thanking you, says my aunty politely.

—You're welcome, I say, equally politely.

—Saoirse, she goes.

—Yes? I go, blandly.

We're not exactly on speaking terms at the moment, my aunty and me.

She sighs.

—Look, Saoirse, she begins, but just then my uncle clatters through the back door and announces that he's taken a notion to have some winkles for his tea and will I go down to the beach to give him a hand.

—*Winkle-picking?* Ah, no way, do I have to?

Winkle-picking is my most hated thing. I can't stand winkles: the slimy greyness of them, and the squishy pulpy feel of them, and the way they have wee bumps all over them like goosepimples.

—Young lady, my aunty goes, sharply. The amount of trouble you're in you'd be as well doing as you're asked and keeping your mouth shut.

—What did your last slave die of? I go.

—None of your guff, she goes. Get your wellies on and go help your uncle. You know how bad his hands get in this

88

weather, she adds in a whisper as he leaves the room to get the big bucket.

I huff as big a sigh as I dare, and I stomp down to the beach after my uncle. The best place for winkles is along the rocky lower north side of the bay, where the beach is pebbly and uneven, and the tide difference is greatest. You find winkles clustered in the rock pools along the water line, and we wade out through the foamy little breakers to pull the best winkles. You can't just tug at winkles to get them from the rocks, or you'll snap them off halfway. You have to dig your nails right in underneath the shell and give a sharp flick of your wrist to prise the winkle from the rock, and you can feel them stretching as you pull. The first, and only, time I ever ate winkles, I couldn't get it out of my head that we were eating slugs, and I kept thinking of the slugs in the vegetable patch in Belfast that my father'd sprinkled with salt until they shrivelled up on their backs.

We work side by side, without speaking. After a bit, we move to the more sheltered west side of the bay. My uncle pauses to have a nip of tea from his flask, and we crouch down in the lee of a sand dune. It's started to drizzle, and the stiff breeze is driving the rain almost horizontally at us.

—Can we go yet? I say.

My uncle glances up at the sky. The clouds are beginning to thicken overhead, and he frowns, and tugs his flat cap lower on his head.

—Let's pull just a few more.

—Do you think there'll be another storm the night?

—Looks like there's one more blowing up all right. Then he turns to me, and he goes, So.

Here it comes.

—So what? I go.

—So, Saoirse, are you and your aunty still at loggerheads then?

—She's way over the top! She's treating it like what I did was a mortal sin. She keeps bargin' the head off of me.

—Ach, you know what your aunty's like. She's only worried about you, love.

My uncle reaches out and cuddles me around the shoulder. I jerk away from him and he looks at me with his big droopy auld eyes. I feel a wee bit bad. He's all right so he is, my uncle.

—I know it's hard on you, he goes. Us old fogeys, ey?

—She says I'm not allowed to go to this party on Saturday night any more.

—I'll have a word with her.

—Will you?

—Aye.

—Thanks. 'Cause I'm not a little girl. And she treats me like I'm still one.

—She just doesn't want you getting in any trouble. You've been doing rightly, with your studies and all.

—I came second in the Irish test.

—You did? He beams. That's my girl, ey?

The rain gets heavier all of a sudden.

—Ach, come on, let's get back, he goes.

We stand up. My uncle's stiff getting to his feet.

—Give us the bucket, I go.

—As I say, he goes, you're a good girl. Just don't let yourself get worked up, and I'll have a word with your aunty. You're right, she's maybe a wee bit harsh on you.

Back at the house, my aunty rinses the winkles under the outside tap and tips them into the big cast-iron pot to boil. I've washed the slightly rancid smell of winkles off my hands

90

and I'm just about to head upstairs to my room when she goes, in a funny voice, Saoirse?

—What?

—You just missed your father, she goes, deliberately casual.

—My father?

—He was on the phone. He said he wants to come down and see you this weekend. Saturday night. Take you out for your dinner.

—What? Why? Sure I'm only after seeing him a couple of weeks ago.

—As I say, I just took the message, she shrugs.

—Ah, no way! It suddenly occurs to me: Saturday night!

—You're not still hoping you can go to that party Saturday, are you? she goes, tersely. Because I've already told you, I don't want you hanging around those Mahon boys. They're trouble, those two, and I don't want you getting involved with them.

I don't say anything, then, because if she so much as suspected anything about me and Johnny Mahon she'd have my guts for garters.

Brid and Michael Deegan arrive with wee baby Seamus, who's only six weeks old. My aunty swoops down on him and picks him up and jiggles him around, and he's sick all down her shoulder, but she doesn't mind.

—He's a wee cherub, she goes, even after he's just boked up on her. She rocks him until he goes to sleep, and then she puts him back in his carry-cot, beside the Aga, and he sleeps all through tea.

Brid and Michael are finding it hard to settle back into Gweebarra Bay, they say. They were living down in Galway, and they moved back up just before Seamus was born to be near Brid's family.

—I met one of the nuns from school, Brid tells us. I was out with my friend Aileen and her wee girl, and we met Sister Alphonso; Phonsie we called her. She started cooing at Seamus in the pram, and congratulating me, and then she turns to Aileen, and says she's sorry. Sorry for what? Aileen goes, and Phonsie goes, Well, and raises her eyebrows at Aileen's Molly in the buggy, and she bends in and whispers that it's hard for the poor child being born *out of wedlock*. Jaysus, I'm telling you Aileen near enough exploded! This is the nineteen eighties we're living in, she goes, not the nineteen feckin' fifties. I thought auld Phonsie was going to drop to her knees there and then in front of the Post Office and start up with the Hail Marys and prayers for Aileen's soul. Brid giggles, but then she stops, abruptly. You know, it is hard on Aileen, alone with wee Molly. She's thinking of moving across the water, to Liverpool maybe. She's got friends live there, and she says it'll be easier on Molly.

My aunty shakes her head slowly.

—Even in this day and age, she goes.

I think, I can't wait to get away.

Later on, the conversation turns to me, and to my Summer Ball, which is coming up in a few weeks' time.

—Have you got a date yet? goes Michael Deegan, winking at me.

I shake my head.

—What! No boyfriends on the scene? I find that hard to believe, a good-looking lass like yourself.

—Ach, she'll have plenty of time for boyfriends, my aunty goes, quickly.

Me and Johnny Mahon have been sort-of going out for a couple of months now. At least I think we're going out. I'm hoping he'll come to the Summer Ball with me. But I haven't brought it up yet, and I wonder how I'll tell my aunty. She's funny about boyfriends at the best of times – she's old-fashioned like that – and she wouldn't take kindly to the news that I was dating one of the Mahons. Two of their uncles from Derry are in the Maze prison up North doing short sentences for possession of firearms and suspected paramilitary involvement, and Aunt Bernadette doesn't trust anyone who's involved with politics.

—Show us your dress, Brid goes.

My ball dress is made out of a beautiful greeny-blue satin that changes colour when the light hits it. It's got a nipped-in waist and a full, ruched skirt. I chose the material myself, and had it specially made by a lady in Dungloe. I love that dress. I've had it hanging on the back of my door for the past week since I picked it up. I put it on and come downstairs to the kitchen.

—Wow! goes Brid. The colour of that goes perfect with that dark hair of yours.

—Aye, that dress is brave and pretty on you, goes Michael.

—Give us a twirl, goes Brid.

I spin round on my tiptoes and the skirt swishes across the flagstone floor. Brid claps, and I strike a pose, and we laugh. But out the corner of my eye I catch my aunty looking at me funny.

—What is it? I say.

—What?

—You were looking at me with a funny look.

—Was I?

—You were, aye! What is it?

—Nothing, love. You just . . . She coughs. Ach, just for a second there, you looked the spit of your mother. Green was Deirdre's favourite colour, too.

Neither of the Deegans says anything.

—I'm going to get changed back now, I go.

—You look lovely, pet, my uncle goes. You look really lovely.

Upstairs, I stuff the dress back on its hanger and bundle it into the wardrobe.

After the Deegans leave, my aunty and uncle and I sit for a while in the living room, watching the news on TV. They start talking about the arms find at Malin Head in January. Malin Head's only a couple of hours from us. My aunty tuts and changes channels.

—It's a few fanatics, she says, angrily. A few fanatics terrorizing the country and giving Irish folk everywhere a bad reputation.

—That's what my father says, I go. But he says it about Ulster and the Protestants.

—Well, she goes. But she doesn't say anything more because she doesn't like my father.

—There has been a grave miscarriage of justice, someone is saying on the next channel.

—For goodness' sake, she snaps at the TV, and she turns it off. Can you not get a moment's peace? she says, to no one in particular.

The phone rings.

—I'll get it, I go, jumping up.

It's Johnny.

—Saoirse! he goes. I'm at the bottom of the lane.

—What? I twist round so I've my back to the room.

—I said, I'm at the bottom of your lane. I'm ringing you from the phone box. You have to come out right away.

—What? Why, what's up?

—Look, I haven't got time to explain and my money's going

to run out. Just get out here as fast as you can, all right?

—It's half ten.

—I can tell the fecking time for myself! Sorry. I didn't mean that. Just – hurry up, all right?

The line goes dead. I put the phone down carefully and walk back to the sofa and sit back down.

—That was Bridget, I go.

—It's late for her to be phoning.

—We've got a History project to be handing in tomorrow and she rang to remind me in case I forgot.

I say it too fast. But neither my aunt nor my uncle even looks up.

I sit with them for a couple more minutes. My hands are sweaty and I can feel my heart thumping away. Then I do a pretend yawn.

—I might head on up to bed now, I go. My voice comes out high-pitched. Neither of them says anything. I do another yawn. Yeah, I'm feeling a wee bit tired, I go. I think I will go to bed now.

—Night then, pet, says my aunty.

I get up and kiss her cheek.

—Night, Aunty.

—Night, love, says my uncle.

—Night.

I close the door and clatter up the first few stairs. Then I tiptoe back down, stepping on the edges where the stairs don't creak so much, and I slip through the hallway into the kitchen, closing the heavy door gently behind me in case it slams in the draught when the back door's open. I grab my shoes from the porch but I don't stop to put them on; I run down the back steps and across the lawn and into the lane where Johnny's car's waiting, the engine running.

He throws the door open for me.

—Jesus, Sha, it took you long enough.

—I couldn't go right away, they'd have got suspicious.

The car lurches forward and I'm thrown against the dashboard.

—What's up, Johnny? Is something the matter?

His hands are shaking. He fumbles in the glovebox and tosses a packet of cigarettes at me.

—Light us a fag, will you, Sha?

—What's up, Johnny?

—What do you mean, what's up? Nothing's up. Will ya just light us a fag for chrissakes?

I light the cigarette and put it carefully between his fingers. He almost drops it his hands are shaking so much. He takes a long hard drag at it, and then another, and he breathes the smoke out like a deep sigh.

—Jaysus. Jaysus.

—Johnny, is anything the matter, like?

—Would you ever give my head peace? I told ya – nothing's the matter.

Neither of us says anything for a bit. We turn out of the bottom of the lane on to the main road and we drive along towards Ardara. Johnny winds the window down and cold drizzle is rushed in on the wind. I hunch down in the seat. I ran out in such a hurry I didn't lift a coat or anything.

—Where are we going? I try to say it all casual, like, but my voice comes out squeaky.

—Nowhere. We're going back to mine, is all.

—Back to yours?

—Isn't that what I'm just after saying? he shouts, slamming the steering wheel with the palm of his hand. Then he turns round and tugs at my hair, like in a playful way. Ach, Sha, I

96

didn't mean to shout at ya. Been a hell of a day, is all. Ya know?

—Yeah, I go. Yeah.

—But here's the thing, right? There's a, a newspaper in the back. Would you get a hold of it and look up what's on at the cinema?

—The cinema? Sure it's way too late for the cinema. It's gone half ten, Johnny, and—

—I didn't say nothing about going to the cinema. Christ, would you just do as I'm asking ya!

I reach round for the paper and find the listings pages.

—Have you found what's on? he goes, impatient.

—I'm looking.

—Anything'll do. Look up that big multiplex in Donegal Town, all right?

I start to read through what's on. But Johnny's getting more and more on edge.

—Aye, anything, anything'll do. Just choose something. And if anyone asks, yeah, if anyone asks, you and me was at the cinema tonight. Got that?

—But what do you mean?

—Jesus, girl, I mean exactly that: if anyone asks you where we've been, we've been at the cinema. We seen a film and we ate popcorn and we drank feckin' Pepsi and then we drove back to mine.

—But I've been at home all evening. With my aunty and uncle. And if anyone asks them—

—They'll not ask them, Sha. Probably nobody'll ask you anything either. It's only in case, all right?

I don't say anything.

—Sha, sweetheart, I'm only asking ya to do me a wee favour, is all. Nothing's up, it's just . . .

We're turning down the lane towards his house. He pulls the car into the side of the road.

—Ach, c'mere. He straightens out my fringe and strokes my cheek with his fingertips. Alright? You're grand, pet. Everything's grand. Me and, eh— He coughs. Me and, and Éamon got into a wee bit of bother earlier on. Down the town, you know? I won't bore you with the details, like. But you know what Éamon's like, he's a feckin' auld maid so he is, and he just panicked a wee bit and he decided we needed to, you know. It's me ma, you know, the way she'd worry and all.

He stops.

—Listen, Sha. Let's go to the cinema tomorrow, all right? I'll pick you up. Proper date, yeah? Fuck it – you know what, we can go for dinner as well if you want. Make a night of it. Would you like that, would ya? Go somewhere nice for dinner and go to the pictures. We'll get ice cream and all, so we will. How d'e like the sound of that then, ey?

—Yeah. It sounds – nice.

—That's my girl. Now, we'll go in, I'll make you a cup of tea, we'll say hi to Mam and then I'll take you back to yours, all right? All right?

—All right.

—All right. He exhales. All right.

Mrs Mahon's just about to go to bed.

—Did you have a nice night, then? she goes.

—Yeah, I lie, weakly. We were at the – cinema.

She doesn't ask any more.

—Well, she goes, don't be too late up, now. School night and all.

Johnny's in the middle of sitting his Leaving Cert and his mam doesn't like him going out. I bet she knows nothing about the big party he and Éamon are having on Saturday, when she and Mr Mahon are away for the night. Half of our year have been invited to that party, and it'll be the talk of the common room for weeks. I don't say to Johnny that I don't think I can go: recently, I've had this sneaking feeling that he's getting bored of me, or at least of how strict my aunty is, of all the hassle and making up excuses. I don't want to admit to him that Aunt Bernadette doesn't like him or his family. Maybe Uncle Brendan can convince my aunty to let me go to the party for a bit after I've had dinner with my father.

Johnny and I hang about the kitchen for five or ten minutes having a cup of tea before he leaves me home, only slightly less jumpy than he was before.

I make it up to my room without my aunty or uncle hearing me. I lie awake for ages, wondering what's going on. The cartoon moons and stars on my wall grin at me. I must decorate my room, I think. What sixteen-year-old has smiley moons on her bedroom wall? I remember when my uncle painted it, when they were doing up the attic box room to be my bedroom. They ran out of paint halfway through doing the sloping ceiling-wall of the alcove where my bed is, and Uncle Brendan had the idea of painting a mural of a night-time sky, and I jumped up and hugged him for the very first time, then. In bed, looking up out of the little skylight in the middle of the cartoon night-time, I can see a patch of real night, with its scattered handfuls of stars. I love the view from my skylight. You can see past the whin bushes and the sand dunes and all across the sweep of the bay. The wind's still up, blowing west across the bay, and dark clouds are scudding across the moon. When I was wee, I used to lie in bed and try to work out which stars were stars and which were really the lights of Faery: torches burning on the battlements of the Castle in the Sky. I haven't thought of that in ages. I sit up and squint at the stars. But they all just look like stars, now; and the more I stare at them, the more I think how they're not even star-shaped; they're just dots, pinpricks in the sky.

13

Saturday night, and the whole world is at the Mahons' party except for me, who's categorically forbidden from going, and so who's the youngest person in the Lounge Bar of Kelly's Hotel by a couple of decades. My father clears his throat and smiles at me. The two of us are just sitting here with nothing to say between us. I try my hardest to think of something else to say. But all I can think about is the party, and how if I'm not there Johnny might find some girl he likes better. Some girl who's prettier, maybe, or more fun, who can make him laugh and not mind if he tells her to pretend they've been to the cinema when they haven't and is always saying the wrong thing. I don't know why Johnny chose me; Johnny Mahon, whom most of the girls in school are after. A couple of months back he just pulled up at the bus stop after school one day and did his cheeky grin and said could he offer me a lift home. I couldn't get over the fact that he knew who I was, let alone where I lived. Bridget stood there with her mouth hanging open and she didn't even have the wits about her to ask if she could have a lift as well, seeing as we live close enough by. Why'd he want to ask you out, then? she said on the phone that evening. Sure you've never even spoken to him before, have you? What on earth did youse talk about, ey?

I can't have been any sort of company; I was the colour of beetroot and the whole way back I was that tongue-tied that anything he asked me I kept getting flustered and answering in yeses and noes. But after that he picked me up from school a couple more times, and we'd go on drives – nowhere in particular, just all over Donegal – and then one evening we went to the cinema in Glenties and afterwards he kissed me and I supposed we were properly going out, then.

—This is nice, isn't it, my father goes, for the second or third time.

—It is, aye, I go, and I try and put a smile in my voice as I say it because I suddenly feel sad for him. He pulls at his beard. He looks tired. His beard is all grizzly these days. I go back to looking at the pot of ferns.

Our table is beside the big fireplace. It's a chilly evening, especially in the draughty auld lobby, but as we're already into June, there's no way they'd light the fire, and there's a big pot of ferns in the fireplace instead. The ferns are old. You wouldn't be able to tell unless you looked closely. But I'm sitting with my back to the room, and the pot of ferns is the only thing for me to look at when there's nowhere else to look.

A lady starts up playing the piano at the other end of the lounge. My father hums along to the tune she's playing. I don't recognize it. It's one of those slow Irish ballads that old men get choked up over.

> —As I was a-walking down by the Lock Hospital
> Dark was the morning and cold was the day
> I spied a young comrade wrapped up in white linen
> Wrapped up in white linen and cold as the clay.

He sings along for a bit. He gets most of the words. Then he breaks off.

—You used to love that song, he goes.

—Did I?

—You did, aye. Used to make you cry.

I don't remember. I don't remember much about that time.

—It was on Christy Moore. *Prosperous*. That was one of our favourite records for a bit. Your mammy and me.

Hearing him talking about him and Mammy makes me feel funny and kind of empty. My father and I never talk about my mother. Never. It's weird hearing him talk about her, about him and her, about *our*.

He's looking at me with his head tilted to one side.

—Oh, I go. What does he want me to say?

—Not that we had many.

—Eh?

—Records. That was one of the first we bought, that *Prosperous*. Seventy-two, I think. Aye, it would be. Would have been. Used to play it all the time. Dance in the living room.

—Really? It's odd to think of my mother and my father dancing around a living room. Were you happy, then? I go.

—Happy? He looks up at the ceiling and puffs his cheeks out. Happy. Aye, I suppose we were, back then. Happy.

—Da, I go, shy now, Da, how did you and Mammy meet?

It's something I've always wondered about: him a Protestant and what's more an RUC man from the North, and her a Catholic girl from the Gaeltacht. It's something I've always wanted to ask, but the subject, or the opportunity, has never really come up before with my father, and I don't know why but I've never wanted to ask my aunty.

He's quiet for a bit.

—Up in Derry, he says, eventually. Summertime. Sixty-eight, it was. Deirdre was marching, the Civil Rights, you know?

—The Civil Rights? Wasn't that dead violent?

—Not at the beginning. Not when I met your mother. It was peaceful in those days. Everyone thought things were going to be better.

—And so how exactly did you meet? Marching?

—No, no, no. At a party. Some party I'd gatecrashed, would you believe. With Jimmy – do you remember Jim? Uncle Jimmy, you used to call him. Bought you a teddy bear for your birthday once. Purple. Horrible thing. Couldn't get it off of you for months.

I shake my head.

—Well, as I say, me and Jimmy gatecrashed this party. We were off duty, out of uniform, you know. Your mammy was having an argument with someone. Fell for her as soon as I saw her. She was the most beautiful girl in the room, so she was. She was wearing this bright green mini-dress and her hair reached her waist.

—Oh, I go.

Derry. Mammy marching in Derry. That's something I wouldn't've thought of.

—Civil Rights was your mother's burning passion.

I wait for my father to go on, but he doesn't say anything more. He joins in the last words of the song:

—On top of his tombstone these words they are written,
'All you young fellows take warning by me,
Beware of the flash girls who walk in the city,
The girls of the city were the ruin of me.'

He whistles and claps when it comes to an end.

—Da-a, I go, embarrassed for him.

He looks at me with crinkly eyes.

—Do you know, he goes, you always used to skip around

singing: *Beware of the flash girls who walk in the city.* You'd have your mother and me in fits.

—Really? I rack my mind for the memory of it. But I can't remember it at all.

My father picks up his pint glass. It's almost empty. He looks at it for a second, and puts it back down.

—Would you like another? he goes.

—You're all right.

—Sure?

I nod.

—A soft drink maybe?

—No thanks.

He gets up and goes to the bar. When he comes back, we neither of us say anything for a bit. He drinks his drink and I fiddle with the beer mat. Uncle Brendan used to collect beer mats, a while back, until he got too many of them and my aunty said they were cluttering the place up. He tried to make them into a decoration for the walls of the guest rooms, sort of like a collage, but she would have none of it. I wonder if he had this beer mat ever. It's one of the old-style Guinness ones, but the toucan's wearing a sun-visor. I think about taking it home to show him, but there's a faint stain of beer on it and one of the corners is a wee bit scuffed. I push it away and look up. My father's watching me with a funny look on his face.

—I hear you got into a wee spot of bother after your hockey match, he goes.

Jesus. So that's it: that's the reason for this out-of-the-blue visit of his. Normally, my da comes down at Christmas, Easter, half-term and my birthday, and I was a bit surprised when my aunty told me he was coming down to take me out for dinner. Why couldn't he just've said something at the start instead of dragging it all out as if this extra visit was fun or something? I shove my chair back from the table and fold my arms.

—Camogie, it was a *camogie* match. Not hockey. Camogie.

—Camogie. There's a quare-sounding word for you, ey? I wonder why they don't just call it hockey.

—Because it's not hockey, it's camogie, that's why.

He was making a joke, of sorts. I realize it too late. There is a slight pause. My father studies the froth stuck to the rim of the inside of his pint glass. He rubs at the rim with one finger, and clears his throat a couple of times.

—Anyways. Sha, I hear a few of youse got yourselves into trouble, am I right?

—Who told you? Did Aunt Bernadette tell you, then? Because it's none of your business, so it's not. And I won't sit here and listen to you telling me off. I won't!

—Love, I'm not about to tell you off. I just want you to tell me what happened.

—I'm sure my aunty told you enough. I should have known you wouldn't want to come up and visit me of your own accord. My aunty told you to come up and have a word with me. Didn't she? She did, didn't she? It wasn't you at all. I should have known. You're pathetic. All of youse are pathetic.

—Here, don't you be speaking to me like that. I'm your father.

—No you're not!

It's away out of my mouth before I can stop it. My father looks away.

—I didn't mean – what I meant was—

—It's all right, love, he says, heavily. Your aunt only mentioned it in passing because she and your uncle were worried, like. I wasn't about to get angry with you. A wee jar now and again is all well and good, but—

He stops, abruptly.

—But what?

—But . . .

—*What?*

—Your mammy got sick from the drink, you see, he says, in a rush. That's all, he adds, feebly, looking up at me quickly then looking away.

Mammy?

A sudden tightness worms its way up my chest and into my throat. I go to speak but my mouth has gone dry. I remember Mammy and Daddy shouting, one night, and a glass bottle being smashed on the kitchen floor.

—Mammy?

And my voice, when it comes, is all croaky.

—That's not true, I go. But my father won't meet my eye.

—I would have known, I go.

He doesn't say anything.

—I would've. Course I would've.

He still doesn't say anything. I laugh.

—Well, that certainly explains why my aunty overreacted and that over the auld camogie match! I go, in a jokey voice. Here, do you want to know what happened, then? Do you? I may as well tell you.

I launch into what happened, a tiny part of me aware that I'm talking too fast.

What happened was this: after the Cup Match a couple of Saturdays ago, when we'd thrashed the Letterkenny team, Mrs Sullivan, the coach, and auld Sister Bartholomew, who was driving the minibus, said we could get fish and chips before heading back. Bridget had got a couple of bottles of Buckfast, and a few of us – me, Katie Malley, Mairead, Aoife and her – downed them in the loos of the sports ground. I wasn't really even that keen, to be honest, but Bridget'd made a couple of snide remarks and so I wasn't going to say no, and besides, I kind of miss having her as my best friend since she's been acting all odd recently. But then Bridget and Katie Malley took off somewhere, and they came back to the minibus almost an hour late and Mrs Sullivan smelt the drink off them and then, twenty minutes into the journey back, Aoife boked up all over the bus and Mrs Sullivan had to clean it up with handfuls of tissue. So the five of us got hauled in front of the Headmistress and letters written to our parents. And when Aunt Bernadette found out, Jesus, was she ever cross; she was that powerful cross, I don't think I've ever seen her so angry.

—I said I was sorry, I go in a rush, but she was ragin'. Like, absolutely *ragin'* and I didn't know why because it was silly and I wasn't even that drunk and . . .

My father is nodding.

—I'm sorry, love. It's only because of your mother. That sort of thing, he goes, awkwardly, it can run in a family, you know?

—Don't be stupid! I go. What are you trying to say?

—Nothing, love, he goes, helplessly. As I say, it's only because of your mother that your aunt's—

—Well, I'm not my mother! I interrupt, and my voice comes out too high-pitched. I'm not – I'm me.

—Of course you are, love.

It is a relief to get home. I don't even care about missing the party any more. My father runs me up from the hotel and he stops at the end of the lane; we sit for a bit, but he keeps the engine running. I want to say something more about my mother. Ask him stuff. But I don't. And he doesn't mention her either, even though I can see he's trying to say something, too. After a while he says, Well . . . and at the same time I say, I'd better . . . and he says, Yes, yes; and then he launches into the usual about how it was good to see me and that if I want a wee holiday I'm welcome to come up North and stay with himself and Pauline. He always says, You're welcome to come up North and stay with myself and Pauline, and I always say, Yes, I maybe will; as if it's scripted; and it's the only time he ever mentions *Pauline* and we both know I won't be going to visit them. Him and his fancy woman whom he married less than a year after Mammy disappeared.

I always used to wonder if Mammy was married to someone else, somewhere, too. But I don't let myself wonder that any more. What became of her. Because she left. She just left. Without so much as a letter of explanation, she just left in the middle of the night one night; and I spent all of my wishes, every single birthday candle I blew out when I was wee, I spent them all wishing that she'd turn up, or that a card from her would arrive. But we never heard anything from her. And now . . . now, it's like I don't know if I'd even recognize her if I passed her in the street.

—So, my father goes, as I say, Pauline'd love to meet you, so you will think about it, won't you, coming up North.

Dream on, is what I want to say, but I just mumble, Aye, maybe, like I always do. But my father knows fine well that what I'm really saying is Take a Long Walk off of a Short Pier, and he sighs. As I'm getting out of the car he says, Give my regards to your aunty and uncle.

—Why don't you seeing as you're so bloody thick with them these days, I say to the closed door, and then I turn and walk fast up the lane. The night breeze is stiff with salt and it tangles my hair across my face and my eyes start to water but I suddenly feel as if I can breathe again. When I get to our gate, he's still sitting there in the car. I can't see past the glare of the headlights, and I don't know if he can see me, but I turn and do a wee wave, and then I unlatch the gate and run down the drive and round the back where the door'll be on the latch for me.

Aunt Bernadette is sitting up by the range waiting for me. I stop on the threshold.

—Did you ask your father in? is the first thing she says.

And all of a sudden I'm sick to death of all the stupid games they play, she and my father. In all the years my da's been coming to visit, he's never once stayed at Gweebarra Sands, even when it's been out of season and there've been all of the rooms free. Mostly he stays at Kelly's Hotel, or occasionally, if it's full, he'll stay in one of the rooms above Logue's. Aunt Bernadette always says have I asked him in, and she always says he's surely welcome, and she always sniffs and raises her eyebrows when I say he's staying at Kelly's, or at Logue's, but we both know that if it came down to it she'd rather die than see him darken her doorstep.

—There's some stew on, if you're hungry, she says.

I shake my head.

—I kept it warm for you.

—And why would I be wanting stew now? Why would I be hungry, ey? Sure, wasn't my father taking me out for my dinner?

—It was just in case, love. I thought maybe he'd've took you somewhere you didn't like the food, is all.

—That was *once*, Aunty, when I was *nine*, and it was only because the people at the table beside us were having snails.

—As I say, it was just in case.

—Well, I had a lovely dinner. We went to this new place up Dungloe way. And then I hear myself adding, spitefully,

And after we'd eaten we went back to the bar at Kelly's and my da bought me a couple of drinks.

—Saoirse, she goes, and then she stops.

—It was you rang him and got him to come up here. I'm not an eejit.

She says nothing.

—That was fly of you, so it was. Ringing my da behind my back. He's *my* da! And then pretending to me that it was his idea. That he actually wanted to come up and see me of his own accord.

We stare at each other for a moment. My aunty is the first to look away.

—Nobody's ever straight with me, I go. There's all of this scheming, and *secrets*; there's all of these secrets, and going behind people's backs, and pretending, and not telling the real reasons for things, and I'm sick of it. It's not fair.

Then I go, So my mother was an alcoholic, then.

My aunty's head jerks up.

—Did your father say that? Her lips are pursed. He had no right—

—Don't you dare say that! Now at least I finally understand why you got yourself so het up over nothing.

—Making yourself sick with drink and getting letters sent home from the Headmistress is hardly nothing, young lady!

—But you overreacted. Admit it! Admit you overreacted because it was in the back of your mind that Mammy was an alcoholic and—

—I am not having this conversation with you, she gulders.

—Yes, yes you are, Aunt Bernadette! I gulder back. Then I take a deep breath and lower my voice. Yes you are. Because I'm not a little girl any more. And because it's to do with me, all right, it's to do with me and I have a right to know.

Suddenly, like something's snapped, she slumps down at the table and takes her head in her hands.

—I'm sorry, pet, she goes.

—Fuck you, I go, shakily. She doesn't look up. Fuck *sorry*, I go again. She still doesn't say anything. Aunt Bernadette? *Aunt Bernadette*, will you look at me? Will you please look at me!

She lifts her head slowly, but she doesn't quite meet my gaze; her face is hanging, and haunted, and – and *fearful*? I stare at her: and yes, she looks unmistakably scared, part of me thinks with surprise. Why would my aunty be looking *scared*?

Blood is thudding in my head. I don't want sorry, I go, in a rush. I just want – not to be always kept in the dark. You know?

—There's just some things, she says, still gazing at the wall behind me, some things that the knowing of them doesn't help you.

—But the not knowing of them is worse, I flash back at her.

There's a long silence when I say that, and neither of us moves. We are frozen into place like statues staring at each other, as if we're illustrating a scene from a story, I think. The only sound is the slight creaking of the porch door where it's not properly shut. I go out of the kitchen and kick the door closed.

—Your uncle'll need to fix that door, my aunty goes when I come back into the kitchen. She stands up abruptly and turns away. Her shoulders are trembling.

—I helped him fix it the other day. He put in new hinges. He says it's the frame itself's warped. And there's probably woodworm. Where is Uncle Brendan?

—Gone to bed. He's up early the morrow to go to the Sligo Farmers' Market with Manus.

—What's Manus doing trailing his few wee spuds all the way to Sligo?

—The sake of habit, I suppose.

She doesn't say anything else for a bit. Her neck is bowed and she's gripping the edge of the sink as if there's a heavy weight on her back. What is it? I want to ask. I swallow, but my throat is closed over and I can't get the words out. Something's not right: there's something else going on here, but I'm suddenly, irrationally, too scared to ask what it might be.

Then, One of these days, she says, finally, without looking up, one of these days we'll sit down, you, me and your uncle, and we'll have a long chat.

My breath catches in my throat.

—Yeah, I say, yeah, and about time too. It's what I wanted, but my legs feel wobbly all of a sudden. Yeah, I say again, too loudly. That's what we'll do. Good, I add, stupidly. Good. Yeah.

My aunty straightens up. Jesus, I think, she looks haggard. She's got old, I think, with a shock.

—C'mere, pet, she goes, and I slide into the seat beside her. She brushes my fringe back from my forehead. Give us a hug, *céadsearc*.

I let her hug me in her bear hug. Then, Aunty, I go into her shoulder, almost in a whisper, Aunty, what do you think happened to Mammy? Where did she go when she escaped? Across the water, do you reckon?

She hugs me even tighter, so tight I can't hardly breathe.

—I don't know, love, she whispers back. I don't know what to tell you.

I wriggle out of her arms. I'm tired suddenly; my whole body feels heavy with tiredness and I don't want to think about anything any more.

—I'm going to bed, I go.

—Good idea, she says. Get yourself on upstairs, then, and I'll bring you up some milk and biscuits.

—Don't be silly, I go. Milk and biscuits.

—I remember a time when you couldn't go to sleep unless you'd had your wee mug of hot milk and your biscuits to dip.

—And how long ago was that, ey?

—It doesn't seem like so terribly long ago. She sighs. Night night, then, love.

The wind has picked up. I lie in my bed and look out of the skylight; dark clouds are racing and tumbling across the bay and hiding the stars. The window is a tiny bit ajar, and the draught is whistling through the gap. I kneel up to close it, and I watch the sea for a while. The waters are choppy and restless; the wind's blowing crossways and the waves are struggling to get to the shore.

I hear Aunt Bernadette on the stairs and I lie back down again. She nudges the door open with her foot and comes in carrying a tray with a mug of warmed milk and a saucer of HobNobs. I roll over and close my eyes as if I'm asleep.

—Ach, Saoirse, love, she says, quietly.

She puts the tray on my bedside table, and she stands there for a minute before leaving the room and closing the door gently behind her.

School the following Monday, and in Registration, Clodagh Mulcahy whispers, loud enough for the people sitting near us to hear, Saoirse! How's the love life, then? Then she sniggers.

I pretend not to hear her but I can feel my ears going red.

—You weren't at the Mahons' party on Saturday night, she hisses, louder.

—No, I wasn't, I go, not lifting my eyes from the Irish grammar homework I'm finishing off. A coldness creeps through my tummy. Clodagh's been after Johnny Mahon ever since her family moved here from Sligo a couple of months ago. Her da is the owner of a couple of new golf courses, and Clodagh gets her highlights done every six weeks and shops in Brown Thomas in Dublin and she's used to getting what she wants.

—So where were you, then? she goes.

—Nowhere, I go.

—There's no need to be so secretive, she goes.

She's got an audience now. Bridget and Katie Malley are tittering and I wonder if Bridget's put her up to something. Bridget used to be my best friend but she's thick as thieves with Clodagh these days.

—So tell us, she goes.

—Tell you what?

Sister Bonaventure still doesn't look up from the roll-book.

—Tell us about your new man, then.

—What?

—Our Seamus says he seen you going into the bar at Kelly's Saturday night with a new man. Does Johnny know you've got a new man? She glances round to see who is listening. An *older* man, she says, smugly. Our Seamus says he looked old enough to be your da.

—It was my da, you silly cow, I snap.

—Saoirse! Sister Bonaventure looks up, frowning. Do you have something you'd like to share with us?

—No, Sister.

—Are you sure now?

—Yes, Sister.

Clodagh Mulcahy turns away and flicks her hair, and as soon as Sister Bonaventure looks away, she and Bridget dissolve into stifled fits of giggles.

As the bell goes for the start of lessons, Clodagh comes up to me, and says, with wide eyes, Saoirse, I'm sorry, I didn't know that about your da. So he's a Protestant from up North is he? That explains your surname, then, I suppose. But how stupid of me. I went over to the Mahons' yesterday to say thanks for the party, and I think I might have mentioned that you'd an older man on the scene, saying as I *assumed* that in that case you wouldn't be wanting to go to the Summer Ball with Johnny after all. Oops-a-daisy!

And she brushes past before I have the chance to say anything. Although what can I say? Even though she's only just started at the school I bet she knows fine rightly that it's my aunty and uncle I live with, that my father's an RUC man from Belfast, that my mother disappeared when I was seven. Tears prickle at the back of my eyes and I blink, hard; furious. It doesn't seem to matter that I've lived here for nearly ten years; it doesn't seem to matter that I'm almost always top of the class in Irish, or that I go to Mass just like the rest of them; none of it matters, because when it comes down to it, even after a couple of months – a matter of weeks, really – Clodagh Mulcahy is less of an outsider than I'll ever be.

14

I don't see or hear from Johnny for a couple of days. I ring the house three times, but his mam answers and says Johnny's not in; the third time I ring I think I hear her stifle a sigh when she says she'll get him to give me a ring back, and so I don't phone again.

Late on Thursday afternoon I'm coming back from Quinnsworth with bags of shopping when it starts to rain: dull rain falling from a thick grey sky. It's the worst sort of weather; the sort of numbing, dreary weather that bores you half to death. And it's a bad sign that it's this dismal and downcast in June, because it means people won't be inclined to come up the coast for the weekend. Every year fewer and fewer guests come to Gweebarra Sands. Nobody wants to stay in a wee family B & B in the middle of nowhere when there're big hotels with subsidized golf links right on site, and horseriding for the kids, and windsurfing and fishing trips and what have you. Around Gweebarra Bay is bleak; dead beautiful, to be sure, but in a very desolate and empty sort of way; in this sort of weather it feels like the loneliest place on earth. I don't think I'll stay here, definitely not for ever, and probably not for very much longer. But any time I wonder about leaving, I think: I don't know where else there is for me to go.

I trudge along the road for a bit, but every time a car goes past it swishes me with water, and so I clamber over the low stone wall to short-cut through Manus Dennehy's back fields, which join up with what used to be the O'Conor farm in the days when it was a farm, before the Dennehys bought the land off my grandparents and my aunty turned the farmhouse into a B & B. Nowadays most of the fields lie fallow; Manus Dennehy's near eighty now, and over the past decade he's worked less and less of the land until these days it's just a couple of fields of potatoes, his flock of sheep and the peat bogs to the east. I often wonder how long he'll be around, and what will happen, once he's gone, to the Dennehy farm without anyone to take it over. Long stretches of the dry stone walls have tumbled to the ground, and the corrugated iron roofs are rusting on the barns, and the grubby outbuildings have broken windows and peeling whitewash. It's like wherever you look, everything's quietly crumbling away.

I clamber up the *cnuceen*, and pause at the top of the ridge to get my breath back. To the right are the deserted barns, and the slough, and the beginning of the peat bog, and to the left are the fields where the gorse is taking over. The bushes are in flower, and the clusters of yellow are the only touch of colour for miles. Under the low blanket of cloud, everything is still. Then, just as I'm about to go down the slope, I catch a sudden movement out of the corner of my eye, over in the direction of the old hay barn. I set the bags down and take a few steps to the right to get a better juke, as my da would say. And I see two men in denim jackets coming out of the barn, the shorter one carrying a bundle of hessian sacking. It's – it can't be, I squint as hard as I can – it's, at least it looks like, Johnny Mahon. What on earth is Johnny doing hanging around that auld tumbledown barn for? I open my mouth to call out to him, but something stops me – that I don't know who the other man is, maybe, or maybe it's that I suddenly think of how funny Johnny's been acting lately – and instead

I grab my bags and slither to the bottom, where they won't see me. I'm sweating, now, and I'm covered in mud. I jog across the fields and cut in round the side of the Dennehy farmhouse, which backs on to our lane. Parked to the side of the lane, half hidden by an overgrown hedge, is Johnny's black Volvo with its nodding dog in the rear windscreen. It was him – is him – back there, for sure. I feel cold all of a sudden. I adjust the shopping bags where the handles are cutting into the palms of my hands, and I hurry inside.

I don't know what to say or who to say it to. Then, the following evening, Manus Dennehy is over to get his tea. He's taken to coming over two or three times a week, lately; his wife died a few years ago and he lives by himself now and my aunty feels sorry for him all alone of an evening in that draughty auld tumbledown farmhouse of his. We eat round the table in the kitchen. For afters, she's made panada, which is sort of like bread pudding. It's Manus's favourite dish from when he was a wee boy, he tells us every time she makes it, and he tells us how once his ma caught him in the larder hoking all of the raisins out of it. He has three helpings, pouring lashings of cream on top and sluthering it up, and he gives the bowl to Rosie to lick. Rosie is Manus's old border collie. She's almost as old as I am, and she's arthritic, and her front legs are going bowed. She's lying quietly in the corner in front of the Aga, and she thumps her tail on the ground when Manus reaches the bowl down for her.

—Ach, you're a good girl, arenten you! Manus goes, and he tells us about the time when Rosie was little more than a puppy and she caught a couple of lads staying in the caravan site trying to set fire to one of the hay bales stacked in the field.

—Manus, I go, slowly, is your farm secure?

—Secure? He looks at me, frowning.

—I just mean . . . like those boys trying to set light to the hay.

—And what made you think of that, now? That was years ago. Sure, why would anyone bother breaking into the farm these days, ey? There's nothing worth anything for them to steal. He chuckles. And if anyone comes up to the farmhouse, auld Rosie'll let me know, won't you, girl? She may be getting on, but there's life in her yet.

—But . . . I try again, but the three of them are looking at me funny, so I don't say any more.

After Manus has eaten his fill of panada, the four of us stay sitting at the big wooden table by the range, and Manus Dennehy rocks back in his chair and starts to fill his pipe.

—D'ye want to press it down? he offers.

—You're all right, I go, and he laughs his wheezy laugh.

—We getting too old for that now, are we?

I used to love watching Farmer Dennehy making up his pipe: tapping the bowl to empty the old ashes out, then taking pinches of tobacco from the red tin he keeps in his inside pocket, rolling them into twists and packing them in. He always did it so solemnly, like it was a ritual of great importance, and he'd offer me the pipe so I could stick my thumb in and press the spongy tobacco down before he lit it.

My uncle gets up to pour them measures of whiskey.

—Just a wee rosiner, then, Manus Dennehy says, taking the glass. Just a small one, and then I'd best be making tracks. Then, right away, despite just saying that about making tracks, he says, Would you like a story?

I giggle. I can't help it. Leaning back in his chair in front of the range, with his legs stretched out and his pipe in one hand and his drink in the other, he's never looked less inclined to be going anywhere. He never leaves before he's had at least three whiskeys. He always says about making tracks, and he always stays until the very last minute.

My aunt shoots me a look. He's been like a grandfather to you, is what her look says. I'll not have you making him feel like he's not welcome here.

I glance at Manus. He's fiddling with his pipe, and his hands, his big clumsy auld farmer's hands with their cracked black nails and calluses, are slightly shaky.

—I'd love a story, I go, to make up for it.

—Ach, I don't want to be boring you, he goes. You've more than likely got a thousand things you'd rather be doing than listening to an old man gabbing on. His eyes are sad.

—I'm not bored, I say. Go on and tell us the story, Manus. I haven't heard any of your stories in ages.

—Only if you're sure, he goes.

—I am, aye!

Uncle Brendan catches my eye and gives me a nod of the head, just a tiny nod.

Manus smiles.

—One of Granda Manus's auld stories, ey?

It was my idea that I called him Granda Manus. When I was wee, I used to follow him about, begging for stories. He knows all the stories of Donegal, and he knows all about the *Síde*.

—Remember the blackthorn bush? he goes. Remember how you liked to hear about the auld blackthorn bush?

—Yeah.

—She always loved to hear about that blackthorn bush, did young Saoirse, he says again, chuckling. The Fairy Fort and the rest of it. Ey?

The first time I met Farmer Dennehy, I was sitting on the stone wall where the back of our garden joins on to the lowest of his fields, watching him plough. There was a gnarled blackthorn bush in the centre of the field, growing on a little raised mound in the earth, and he took care to stay about five metres clear of it on all sides. I watched him going round and round in awkward circles instead of ploughing straight, and he saw me watching, and he called over that the reason was the mound was a Fairy Fort.

—Really? A *real* Fairy Fort? I couldn't believe it. So that's where the *Síde* live, is it?

—You know about the *Síde* then?

—Yes, and I know someone who's gone to Tir-nan-Og, I remember saying. I was convinced, you see, I was utterly convinced that I'd find a way to bring Daisy back.

I was a shy wee thing in those days; my aunty says you'd've been hard pressed to get two words out of me, but as soon as I saw the man with the bristly grey beard who looked exactly like King Conchubar out of my story book, and as soon as that man mentioned the *Síde*, I was enthralled. He sat down beside me on the wall, then, and told me how his grandfather had known someone who dug up the tree on a fairy mound, and how, year after year, that man's crops failed. No other farm in the area was blighted, but that man's potatoes turned to black slime in the earth, and his grass withered before it could be made into hay, and one by one his sheep took sick and died, and eventually he was forced to sell up and move away, all because he was foolhardy enough to disregard a Fairy Fort.

—Saoirse! Are you away with the fairies? Manus Dennehy asks, and I blink.

—I was just thinking.

—Well, shall we have this story then or what?

—Yeah.

—Well, Manus goes, planting his elbows on the table and leaning forwards, I was thinking that you might like to hear the story of Roan Inish?

Roan Inish is a very small island, little more than a clump of rocks, just outside of Gweebarra Bay, and you can see it clearly on a good day. In Irish, it means Seal Island.

—There was a dead seal on the beach after the storm last week, I blurt out, remembering suddenly.

—There was? He sucks at his pipe. That's a bad omen. I wonder what it means.

—Manus, says my aunt.

He shakes his head slowly, but he doesn't say any more.

—Are you telling this story, then? goes my uncle. He leans over and refills his and Manus's glasses.

—Roan Inish. Manus clears his throat. There was a time when most people round here made their living from fishing. They lived and died by the sea, and they understood the sea; they had a deep fear of it and a great respect for it. That's not the case any more, of course, and a lot of the ways and wisdoms have been lost over the years. Superstitions, some will say, nothing but old superstitions; but there're others that still believe the worst thing a man can do is harm a seal. To be sure, it's terrible bad luck on your boat if you happen to catch one in your net by mistake, even, let alone actively doing a seal harm. There've been good, sturdy boats gone down in calm waters, and every man aboard drowned, not long after those same men have killed a seal for its skin, or found one tangled in their nets and not released it for fear of losing their catch. By the same token, there're people as say you should never rescue a drowning man: if the sea wants you it'll claim

123

you, they say, and many a rescued man has been turned in the head; he'll long for the sea, he will, a deep and crazed longing for the sea will take a hold of him, and sooner or later he'll return to it, for good.

Manus Dennehy pauses to knock out his pipe and refill it. He doesn't say anything while he's doing it, and nor do any of us. I cross my arms on the table and lean my head on them. The heat is making me sleepy. Manus lights his pipe and takes a long pull at it and starts into the story proper.

—Now, long ago, there was a man who lived among these fisher folk. He was up early one morning to catch the dawn tide, and as he was checking the knots of his fishing nets, he noticed a seal come ashore, and disappear behind a sand dune. He thought nothing of it, one of those things, you know, that your mind notices but you don't pay any heed of, until he saw a beautiful girl sliding down the near side of the dune. Now, whilst he might not pay any attention to a seal, no red-blooded man is going to ignore a beautiful girl, and my Lord she was beautiful, this girl: she was slim with long legs and shiny hair the colour of wet seaweed. And she had not a stitch of clothing on her, not a stitch! This young man was turned instantly weak by the beauty of her, stricken with love in the moment that he saw her slipping naked down that sand dune and dancing into the field. He dropped his nets and scrambled up over the sand dune, and what on earth did he find?

—Her skin, I go, on cue.

Manus twinkles at me.

—Indeed he did! It was a thick, grey, leathery-looking coat, and like oily velvet it was to the touch. He snatched it up and took his own sou'wester off to bundle it up in, and he clambered back over the dune and stuffed it into the stern of his boat, under the lobster-pots. Then he watched, and waited. As the sun came up, the seal-girl – for that she was, of course, and as soon as our young fella'd seen her skin he'd recognized her for a selchie – the seal-girl came back to slip into her skin, but it was gone, of course. She ran down the beach looking for it, and she didn't see the young man until he was almost upon her, and he threw his jumper over her shoulders, and once he'd done that, she was in his power. And they got married, this strange girl and the young man, and he gave up the sea and took to farming, and they moved inland, and they even had a babby son. But one night, a fierce storm blew in off the sea, taking some of the thatch off of the roof of their cottage, and the next morning, the seal-girl saw a bundle of waxed cloth that had been stuffed in under the rafters, and she knew that it was her skin. Now, once a selchie finds its skin, nothing can keep it from the sea; and even though this girl had come to love her husband and her wee babby boy, the pull of the sea was too strong, and she ran across the fields until she came to the Bay and she slipped into her skin and became a seal again. Her husband, coming in from the plough, saw the open door and heard the babby crying and he knew immediately what had happened, and he also knew there was nothing, nothing he could do about it. Thenceforth he was crazed with grief, and he would row out to Roan Inish with the babby in a wee wicker basket in the bow of the boat, and they'd spend hours sitting on the beach, watching the seals, and not knowing that one seal with big sad velvety eyes would slide in close to the shore and watch them, too, caught between the land and the sea, happy to glide amongst the rolling waves but sometimes yearning for the feeling of an eiderdown heavy on your skin on a cold night, or the warmth of a babby on your breast.

He falls silent.

I remember the first time I heard the story of Roan Inish, and I burst out with questions, wanting to know if the man had found a way to bring the seal-girl back.

—No, Manus said, in a strange, tight voice. She never came back.

—Didn't she want to?

—Aye, well, there's powers stronger than want or will, and the kingdom of the sea had claimed her.

Like Tir-nan-Og, I thought, then; like the Castle in the Sky, where Daisy was; and I asked Manus if you could rescue someone enchanted to the sky.

We were on the beach, and I remember how he swept his arm in a wide arc, pointing out at the sea.

—Look, Saoirse, look! Don't you see how, if you look out far enough, the sea and the sky are one?

—Wake up, pet. My aunty is shaking my shoulder. You're drifting off.

—It's late, says Manus Dennehy, apologetically, and he stands up awkwardly. I'm sorry to have taken up your evening so.

—Manus, you belong here as much as we do and you know that.

He and Uncle Brendan trudge off to check on the sheep. Manus doesn't say why he wants to go check on the sheep at this hour, but I know it's on account of that dead seal I mentioned.

I give my aunty a hand with the washing-up.

—He's quare superstitious, auld Manus, isn't he? I go. It really bothered him, hearing about that seal, didn't it? And when he told his story, I thought he was going to start crying a couple of times. His voice went all quavery.

—Ah, Saoirse. It's his own mother drowned when he was a babby, my aunty goes, quietly.

—What? Are you serious? I didn't know that. Why did I never know that?

—The past's the past, she says, in a funny voice.

I start to say, What's that supposed to mean, but halfway through saying it I stop. I'm not sure I want to know any more.

15

Sunday afternoon, and there's a group of us in Melly's playing pool and watching the rugby. Ireland are getting thrashed and as the match goes on the fellas' moods get worse and worse. Johnny especially is taking it badly, punching the table when we miss an easy penalty. He's chain-smoking as well, lighting one B & H off another, and at one point, when Éamon leans over and says something quietly in his ear, he goes white and then red and I think he's going to hit his brother. Johnny hardly speaks to me, and I spend most of the afternoon chatting with Mairead and Aoife. As soon as the match is over, Johnny and Éamon stand up, and Johnny downs the rest of his pint and puts on his jacket.

—Johnny, I say, going over to him, where are you off to?

—Have to go. Wee errand.

—Oh. Just I – I haven't seen you in ages.

—Yeah. Been busy, like.

—I thought I saw your car the other day.

—What other day?

—Thursday. Early evening.

—I didn't go anywhere on Thursday evening. Didn't go out at all, in fact, so it couldn't have been me, Sha. Where d'ye think you seen it anyways?

—Oh, I go, flustered, At the, uh, bottom of the lane.

—Sure what would I be doing at the bottom of your lane if I wasn't calling for you ey? he says, easily. There're loads of black Volvos around. You must have been mistaken.

—Yeah, I go. Must've been.

—Ey! You don't think I'm cheatin' on you, do ya?

—No.

—Well, there you are then. He looks at me for a second.

—Ey, Johnny, goes Éamon, waiting by the door.

—Have to go. See you around, Johnny goes, and he pulls the collar of his jacket up and ducks through the low door.

Bridget's been watching.

—See ya, I call, as casually as I can, and I go back to playing pool for a bit, but I don't stay long after that.

It's been raining off and on all afternoon, and when I leave Melly's the rain's falling steady and heavy from a low blanket of clouds that seems to have settled in for the night. I cut across the fields, and by the time I'm back at Gweebarra Sands not only am I soaked to the skin but my shoes are thick with mud and cow clap. I go in the back way, and take my shoes off in the porch. There's a heap of old newspapers by the back door and I hunker down to scrape some of the clabber off my shoes. The door into the kitchen is slightly ajar, and through it I can hear my aunt and uncle talking. The wind's whistling round the house and rattling the old wooden frame of the porch, and the auld door's clattering again despite the new hinges, so they mustn't have heard me come in. There's an odd tone to my aunt's voice, sort of hysterical, and all of a sudden I realize they're talking about me. I set the shoe and bit of newspaper down and listen, my chest tight.

—She's too young, Brendan!

—Bernie, she's not a child any more.

—Aye, but she gets on like a child.

—Only because you treat her like one.

—*I* do? What do you mean, *I* treat her like a child?

My aunt's voice is shrill. Through the crack in the door I can see her slamming her hands on the table.

—Brendan, to look at the way she acts you'd think she was fourteen or fifteen sometimes. I don't know where I am with her. One minute she's taking herself off for hours on end saying she's going for a walk – going for a walk indeed, as if I was born yesterday, I'd like to know what she really gets up to! – and the next she's drinking herself sick on fortified wine!

—She's a teenager, love. Just a normal teenager.

—No, Brendan, she's not, and that's the problem.

My uncle crosses over and takes my aunt by the shoulders.

I wait for a bit, not daring to move, but neither of them says anything else. And then I realize, shit, I'm trapped. If my aunt turns her head just a fraction I'll be right in her line of vision.

I take a deep breath. Then I inch backwards and open the back door quietly and bang it closed as if I'm just in.

—Hiya! I call, loudly, hoping my voice doesn't sound too false. I'm back!

My heart's yammering away somewhere between my ears. The pounding of it is all I can hear. I take another breath and then I go through into the kitchen. My aunt gets up quickly from the table. She looks dead guilty when she sees me, and I catch her glancing swiftly at my uncle: Do you think she heard? He gives the tiniest shake of his head.

—Saoirse, she goes. Hello. Then she fashions her face into a smile and says, brightly, Did you get your schoolwork done, then?

—Yeah.

—Good. That's good.

—Yeah.

—Well.

The three of us are standing in a triangle, me at the door, my aunty over by the range, and my uncle at the sink. My uncle is running the tap. He's got it turned to full and the water is crashing around the sink and splashing up on to the draining board.

—Brendan, my aunty goes.

He looks up, and looks back at the water, and blinks. Then he takes a glass from the draining board and fills it and turns the tap off. He stays gazing out into the garden, and he doesn't drink the water.

—I'm going to go up and – and finish off my essay, I mumble. Get it written up neatly.

—Grand. I'll call you down when it's time for your tea.

—Yeah.

—Is there anything in particular you'd like for your tea the day?

—No. Thank you.

—How's about some sardines? Manus dropped us over some fresh. I thought we'd have them with some new baby spuds.

—All right.

—You like that.

—Yeah. Thanks.

—Right.

—Yeah. I'll, em, go get the essay done then.

—Right you are. I'll call you when tea's ready.

—OK. Thanks.

I start to go up to my room, but only a few steps up I turn, and go back down, and through the heavy stained-oak door that leads to the guest part of Gweebarra Sands. I wander through the hallway, running my fingers over the books in the bookshelf: they're mostly left-behinds – murder mysteries and trashy detective stories and Readers' Digests, and a couple of books on local flora and fauna and fishing. I adjust a couple of paintings where they're hanging crookedly, and stir up the surface of the pot pourri. We haven't had any visitors since the Easter holidays, and the thick carpet and dark panelled walls smell slightly damp with not being lived in. Patches of wallpaper are peeling slightly; I pick at the edge of a strip where it's curling away from the wall, and then I try and smooth it back down. I stare at my face in the big gilt-framed mirror that's hung on the wall by the front door; I look back at myself, pale and pinched and serious in the gloomy light. Then I turn and go up the stairs and right along the corridor to the smallest guest room, which faces north at the gable end of the house. There's never much sun gets in this room; even in the summertime there's only ever a pale, watery sort of light. Aunt Bernadette puts people in here only if all of the other rooms are taken. Sheets and pillowcases are folded neatly on the bed, ready to be put on for when the season starts. They are cold to the touch, a wee bit clammy. I perch on the edge of the bed and look around the room.

When my mother and I arrived at Gweebarra Sands, we slept in this room, together in the single bed. My aunt and uncle had put up a camp bed for me, but it took up most of the space on the floor, and you'd to fold it up and balance it against the wall every morning. It was the stiff, old-fashioned sort with rusty metal coils and hinges that needed to be clipped shut, and some nights my mother wouldn't be bothered to make it up, or she'd forget, and I'd slide into bed beside her, moulding myself around her back. I liked it better that way. When she left, I carried on sleeping in the smallest guest room for a couple of weeks, until my uncle moved the boxes out of the front attic to make a bedroom of my own for me. I didn't like the guest room. The furniture is of the sort people say has seen better days: dark mahogany, heavy and ornate, and a wee bit shabby, as if it belongs to another room in another time. There is a wardrobe with clawed feet, and a matching bureau, battered, with deep scratches running down one side and patches of flaking varnish on the top. It has an oval-shaped swinging mirror with a border of carved roses, and you can't ever balance it to sit straight; that mirror leans right back to reflect the tops of the walls and the ceiling or else it tilts all the way forwards. There are black spots all over the mirror like sooty finger marks.

I get up from the bed and push the mirror with one finger. It still squeaks. I go to the wardrobe, and open one of the doors; a few metal hangers rattle and the draught sends a sheet of clothes-paper wafting to the floor. I pick it up and slide it back into the top shelf. My mother unpacked hardly any of our clothes when we were here, and everything stayed jumbled up in suitcases under the bed: I must've worn the same jeans and jumper that we travelled in for near on a fortnight. My mother took the ballerina box back off me, on account of how it had a lock, although I never knew what she wanted to lock away in there; and my crayons and books were in the top drawer of the bureau. Any time I left a crayon lying out she would tell me off for messing the place up: we're guests here, she said. Guests. Being guests meant that I wasn't allowed to touch the swinging mirror, or any of the seashells on the windowsill. There were twelve of them, I seem to remember, twelve of them all in a row, little pink and green snail-shaped ones, white spiked conches, and half of an oyster shell, with barnacles on the outside and mother-of-pearl on the inside. Today, there are seven shells still on the ledge. I count them, lifting them one by one, blowing the thin layer of dust off each of them and setting them back carefully, exactly as they were. I remember kneeling on the velvet-covered stool to look at them, and I remember the way I counted them again and again; how someone had arranged them in order of size. But I wasn't allowed to lay so much as a finger on them because they weren't mine and it wasn't my room.

I don't like going into this guest room to clean. I always leave it till the last. All I remember about my first few weeks in Gweebarra Sands is that room; the interminable days when I'd finished colouring in the pictures in my colouring-in books, and I was bored of reading to Emily, and Mammy just lay in bed, not moving, not speaking, just staring at the ceiling.

I wonder whatever happened to my mother; where she went. She ran away to start a new life across the water, and nobody ever heard from her again. At first, I used to believe she'd come back some day, and I don't know at what point I ceased believing that, or stopped thinking about it.

My train of thought is broken by my uncle's voice, thin and faraway, calling me for tea. I jump up, almost guiltily, and look quickly around the room once more. I check my expression in the mirror. I look normal enough.

I leave the room, closing the door carefully behind me, and go back downstairs.

That evening, my aunt and uncle tell me how my mother was an alcoholic; how they tried to look after her by themselves in Gweebarra Sands but how in the end things got so bad that they had to check her into a psychiatric clinic in Sligo. When she came back, she wasn't the same, my aunt says; she was jumpy, and distracted; it was as if, in her head, she'd left us already. She talked of starting a new life, across the water, maybe.

—And then one night, my aunt says, staring at an imaginary point in the air, she threw a few things in a holdall and left without saying a word.

We are back on familiar territory. I finish the story for her: And you've always said you don't know where she ended up.

—No, my aunt says. We never found out.

When I was little, just after Mammy went missing, I spent ages spinning an old globe of the world and choosing, at random, countries where she might have gone. Every time I thought of a new place, I would run to find my aunty: What about India? I'd ask. Or Africa? We heard about India and Africa in church; how there were hundreds of starving orphans there in need of people to help them.

—But, like – England? I muse aloud. Or, or Scotland? Or America, or – where? Seriously, Aunt Bernadette, where do you think she *did* go in the end?

—She just left! my aunty says, helplessly. I can't—

—But you must have some idea, I say, half-heartedly.

I've asked this question so many times before. I don't know why I thought that this time the conversation would go differently. They both shake their heads, and look helplessly at me. And the truth is, a mother who can abandon her daughter, her own, only daughter—

Except that I wasn't my mother's only daughter.

I stand up from the table. I can't talk to my aunt and uncle about it any more. I've never admitted to them – to anyone – how Daisy died.

It has been awkward, embarrassing, even, to hear about my mother and alcohol and psychiatric clinics; my aunt and

uncle are as ill at ease as I am, and I can sense their relief
when I bring the conversation to an end. It's only later on
that I start to feel frustrated that I didn't ask more questions;
questions not about *what* happened, but *why*; about why
things started to go wrong in the first place. Sadness creeps
over me like a feeling of damp that I can't shake off; my
mother feels more distant than ever.

At first, I can't bring myself to go through everything for a
second time with my father, and so I decide to look through
the local newspaper archives in Gweebarra's Public Library
to read up on the Civil Rights. Civil Rights was your mother's
burning passion, my father said, and I know next to nothing
about the marches and that whole era. After school one day,
I get off the bus in town. Mairead gets off too: she wants me
to look at shoes for the Ball with her. I don't admit to her
what I'm doing. I just say, I can't.

—Why not?

—Just stuff, I go. I've just got stuff to do.

—Jesus, Sha, you're acting dead weird these days, Mairead
goes, annoyed.

I shrug, and she goes to walk away. Then she turns, and
says, hesitantly, Sha, it's not – is something wrong, with
Johnny, like?

I shake my head. If I was going to confide in anyone about
Johnny's weird behaviour, it would be Mairead, but her mam
and Johnny's mam are first cousins and I don't want anything
getting back to Johnny.

—Are you two . . . are you still going out?

—I don't know. I think so.

—Here, you're not worried you're – *pregnant* or anything,
are you?

136

—What? No. No. We haven't—

—Cause if something's wrong, you can tell me, yeah?

—Yeah, I go. Thanks. Thanks, Mairead. And I walk off quickly and turn the corner before she can say anything more.

Presiding over the local library like a shrivelled auld lioness is Miss Deeny, who used to be Headmistress of the primary school I went to. She taught there for over forty years, teaching a couple of generations of the same families: she taught my mother, and she taught Aunt Bernadette, and she was probably wearing the same brown tweed skirt and high-necked frilled cream blouse then, too. I can't stand Miss Deeny.

I remember sitting on a brown plastic chair in the corridor of what was going to be my new school while Aunt Bernadette talked to Miss Deeny, who, she said, was going to be my new teacher. I knew that the reason they'd told me to sit outside was because they wanted to talk about me without me listening. But I was used to earwigging on grown-up conversations. I slipped down from the chair and tiptoed across the corridor, and, as slowly and carefully as possible, I turned the handle and inched the door open the tiniest fraction.

—So she's had no religious instruction at all, then? Miss Deeny was saying. I'd already decided that I didn't like Miss Deeny. She was old, with papery skin and gold glasses on a chain that looped behind her ears. She had a big gold brooch in the shape of a lizard at the neck of her frilly cream blouse, and her tights were wrinkled at the ankles.

—None whatsoever, my aunt was saying. My sister's husband, you see.

—I see. Well, Bernadette, you'll understand, I might not

be able to put Deirdre's daughter in with my other seven-year-olds. They're all preparing to make their first Holy Communion, you see.

—I understand, Miss Deeny. But the sooner she settles in and makes friends her own age the better.

Miss Deeny sighed.

—She's had no instruction *whatsoever*?

—As I say, none at all.

Miss Deeny sighed again.

—I suppose, Bernadette, that I could take the child for an hour after school, on Wednesdays, say, and instruct her myself.

—That would be very good of you, Miss Deeny. We'd be very much obliged.

Aunt Bernadette said something else, very quietly, that I didn't catch. Then, through the crack, I saw her turn towards the door, and I skidded back across the corridor and into the brown chair again.

A cleaning lady mopping the tiled floor, working her way down the corridor from the other end, paused and winked at me.

—Are you in trouble, so? Teacher talking to Mammy in there?

I shook my head.

—Cat got your tongue, ey?

—No, I whispered. This is my new school.

—Your new school, is it? And where are you from? You've a funny accent.

—Belfast, I whispered, even quieter.

—Belfast? You're from Belfast? She crossed herself. Ah, Heaven help us all. You'll be much better off out of that hell-hole. Good luck now, ey?

Then Miss Deeny appeared at the door and asked me to

come into the classroom. First of all, she opened a book and asked me to read a story out loud from the beginning. It was easier even than my old Peter-and-Jane books, I remember. She took the book back off me when I was only halfway down the first page, and she opened it further on in.

—Try this, then, she said, frowning over her glasses at me.

I couldn't say the first word.

—*Ay-oh-eef*, I tried. *Ay-oh-eff-ee and her cat*—

—Eee-fah, dear, *Eee-fah*, said Miss Deeny.

—Is it a girl's name? I whispered.

Miss Deeny looked at Aunt Bernadette.

—It's an Irish name, like yours, said Aunt Bernadette. We don't say *Say-oy-arse*, do we now, we say *Seer-sha*. It's an Irish spelling.

—She doesn't have any Irish? Miss Deeny said.

—I know Cúchulainn, I said.

—But can you speak Gaelic?

Mammy was teaching me and Daisy to speak Irish, but we hadn't got very far.

—What about your Multiplication Tables? Do you know your Multiplication Tables?

—You mean my Times Tables?

It was this year in school I was supposed to be learning my Times Tables. Mammy had bought a cassette tape for me, with a woman singing the Times Tables on it, and we'd been playing it and singing along for the first few weeks of summer.

—She's very advanced in Reading and Arithmetic. I must say this makes things awkward, Miss Deeny said. It's a very awkward situation all around. Saoirse will be living with you now, Bernadette?

My aunty squeezed my hand, and nodded.

—Well, Bernadette, as I say, we'll just have to muddle through. Make the best out of a sorry situation. How is, eh— She glanced at me, and stopped. I'll be seeing you tomorrow morning, then, Saoirse.

As we left, she called out, Oh, and one last thing: is Saoirse to be known as O'Conor or Pentland now?

—Pentland, said my aunty. Sure I'm not an O'Conor any more either, Miss Deeny.

—Quite right, Bernadette, quite right. How time flies. It doesn't seem yesterday that Deirdre was Saoirse's age.

As it turned out, I only went for Religious Instruction with Miss Deeny the once. We sat in the empty classroom and she started talking about the Little Jesus Child and Heaven and then she bent towards me with her pale, powdery face, and she said, So would you be missing your little sister then?

I remember noticing that she had a light brown wart on the underside of her chin, with a thin white hair growing from it. I must have stared and stared at that wart.

—Is that what it is, Saoirse? she said, and she asked me if I'd like to talk about it.

—No thank you, I said.

—Now, Saoirse, let's not be bold, she said. Would you please look me in the eye when I'm talking to you! That's better. Now. What do you want to tell me about your sister?

—Nothing, I remember whispering.

—Come now. What was her name?

—Her name's Daisy.

—Daisy?

I nodded.

—Well, Saoirse, Our Lord in His Heaven must have wanted Daisy to brighten His day. You must think of her, up there, smiling down at you.

I remember exactly what I said: Daisy always wanted to go to the Castle in the Sky.

—Well, dear, that's where she'll be.

—She wanted to be Queen of Faery.

—Fairies? No, dear, there's no fairies. Big girls of seven don't believe in fairies any more. Angels, you must mean. Yes, that's right, if you ever feel sad you must think of your little sister up in Heaven with the angels looking after her, sitting at Our Lord's feet. Suffer the little ones to come unto me, He says.

She didn't suffer, Mr Pentland. It was over quickly.

—Daisy didn't suffer! She didn't!

—That's what we call a figure of speech, dear.

I remember sitting there, and the feeling of tears swelling up in my eyes; and I cried for the first time since Belfast. I must have been inconsolable; and once I'd started crying I couldn't stop, and even though I told myself that Daisy *would* be back, that I *would* find a way to bring her back, just like Emer, just like Sleeping Beauty, just like in all the stories, a little part of me didn't believe it any more.

For the first, and only, time I can remember, shy, softly spoken Uncle Brendan put his foot down and categorically stated that I would be receiving no more one-on-one instruction from Miss Deeny; that Sunday School would be more than adequate and there was no need for me to make my Holy Communion until I was quite ready. Miss Deeny never liked me after that, and for the four years that I spent at Holy Trinity Primary School, she referred to me as our little Protestant girl.

Miss Deeny frowns when I walk into the library.

—What can I do for you, Miss Pentland? she says, sniffily. Or are you content to stand there all afternoon?

The auld cow. There's no way I'd let her guess what I'm doing.

—I'd like some history books, I say. About the Civil Rights Marches.

—The Civil Rights?

—Up in Derry. In sixty-eight and that.

—My dear, I'm perfectly aware of when the Civil Rights Marches were, thank you.

I clench my jaw and don't say anything.

She taps at her computer with one finger, then copies down some reference numbers in pencil.

—These are the shelves where you'll find the books.

—And I'd like to look up newspaper archives, but I want papers from the Civil Rights up to the present day.

Without saying a word, she slides a leaflet on *How To Use Microfiche* across the counter.

—Thank you, Miss Deeny, I singsong. She narrows her eyes at me.

I look at the books first. There are only three: one is a collection of essays, and the other two are general histories of the Troubles, both of which have a chapter or two on NICRA and the Derry marches. But it's the photographs I'm interested in. I stare at the grainy black-and-white reproductions and see if I can spot my mother anywhere. But all of the girls in the pictures look pretty much the same; all of them are young, and a lot of them have long, loose hair, and they all have similar expressions on their faces. Any of them could be my mother.

I spend about an hour scrolling through various newspapers on microfiche, but I don't find a single thing about my mother. I choose dates as accurate as possible to when she went missing, and I put her name in the search engine, but

I can't find my mother anywhere. Then, just as I'm about to call it a day, I do one last, open-ended search of the picture archives of the smallest local newspaper. It comes up with one hit: for May 1967. Suddenly I can't breathe. I click on the link: and slowly, line by line, Deirdre O'Conor, aged sixteen, Rose of Donegal for the second year running, appears on screen, wearing her floral wreath and pouting at the camera, and I don't know whether to laugh or cry.

16

I decide, reluctantly, that I'll just have to ask my father out-right about what really happened to my mother. We haven't talked about her for years; we've got used to carefully constructing our conversation around her without ever mentioning her. I use the payphone at the end of our lane to phone Belfast. Luckily, it's my father who answers; if it was Pauline, I'd've hung up right away. But it's my father, and so I say, will he come up as soon as possible, there're things I want to ask him, and he pauses for a bit and then he says how in actual fact there's something he's been wanting to ask me himself, and so if it suits me he'll drive up this weekend.

It's a nice evening, and we drive out to this restaurant my da has read about that's up near Gweedore. We talk mostly about silly stuff, like what I'm doing at school and that, and it's not till we've nearly finished eating that I say to him how I heard my aunt and uncle talking about my mother and that I want to know what's going on.

He doesn't say anything for ages when I say that.

—I need to know, Da, and you have to tell me. You have to! I'm not giving up, you know. I'm not.

My da chuckles.

—What's so funny?

He chuckles some more.

—Seriously, what's so funny? Why are you laughing at me, ey?

—Well, love, don't take this the wrong way now, but for all of your, shall we say, your Celtic upbringing, there's still a good wee bit of the Ulster Prod in you, you know.

—What's that supposed to mean?

—Listen to yourself: here's you. I'll not give in. No surrender! No surrender, ey?

—Da!

—Your great-grandpa was killed on the Somme, you know. Did you know that?

I didn't. I shake my head.

—He was in the famous auld thirty-sixth Ulster Division. Went over the top on the first of July. Most of 'em were wearing their sashes and they went over shouting: For God and Ulster.

—They were – Orangemen?

—Aye, a fair few. By no means all of them. But your great-grandfather was, and in actual fact he was quite high up in the Lodge. It was respectable in those days. Here, do they learn you about any of that in your History?

—Sort of. Not really.

—Out of seven hundred men in his battalion, only about seventy came back. Seventy. Out of seven hundred. The rest . . . And among them, the dead, your great-grandpa William Stanley Pentland and three of his four brothers, all in the one day.

My father suddenly stops laughing.

—Can you imagine that, now. My own father, Stanley Junior – and you know, he was always called Stanley Junior, even when there was no Stanley Senior – he was no more than a toddler, then. And my grandma, she used to tell me how when she got the telegram, she went to her mother-in-law's house just up the road. You could see the sea from there.

Strangford Lough. It was a hot day. And they sat out in the garden, with my daddy just a wee babby playing on the grass, and you know, my grandma always used to talk about how even though it was a calm day, no wind, no wind at all, the waters kept on rippling like something was agitating them. And while they were sat there thegether, the other telegrams came, one by one. My grandma used to say how they saw the telegram boy coming, and there were telegrams for people all along the street, and three times he stopped at their house. Four out of five brothers killed. Wee manila envelopes with *We regret to inform you* . . . I've still got my grandfather's one in the house somewhere. If you're ever interested in that part of your history I'll post it up to you. There's a medal as well. I think I've still got that, too.

—Da, I go, after a bit. Da, see, this is exactly what I mean.

—What's that, then?

—All this! There's all of this – this stuff, you know? Like that happened and all. And I don't know any of it. And how am I supposed to . . . I don't know, you know, how am I supposed to do anything when I don't know any of it?

I push my plate away from me. I'm not hungry any more. It's as if I started out wanting to find out about my mother, but instead of finding things out all I've discovered is a whole load of other things I don't know.

I try to say this to my father.

—I'm sorry, love, he says.

—That doesn't help. I need to know things.

—I know. I'm sorry. Then, without looking at me, What is it you want to know, love?

—Stuff about Mammy.

—Look, he goes, awkwardly. Look, Saoirse . . . He trails off, and sighs. What kind of stuff, he says, quietly.

—Anything. I don't know anything. I only know stupid things like she was a Rose of Donegal two years running.

—She was a Rose of Donegal, was she? he says, with surprise in his voice.

—Two years running.

—Was she now?

—Da, I go, impatiently.

—I didn't know that. She never told me she was a Rose of Donegal. But I can well believe it. What age was she?

—Fifteen, then sixteen. But Da! Listen to me! I want to know real things. I want to know who she was, and what she was like.

He looks at me, helplessly.

—Like, for example, I go, taking a deep breath. You said you met at a Civil Rights thing, yeah? At a party.

—We did, aye. My father shifts from side to side in his seat. —Saoirse—he goes, but I carry on over him.

—But she was a wee Catholic girl from round these parts and you were, what were you, like a policeman?

—A 'B' Special.

—Yeah, that's it. And so how on earth did you, you know, when you both found out that you were, like, on different sides, how did you start going out?

—Ach, it wasn't like that, you know?

—What wasn't like what?

—Well, it was . . . What I mean to say is, and I'm ashamed to say this, love, but it made it more – romantic, sort of thing. More for your mother, I think. She was – Deirdre was . . . She wouldn't let anyone tell her what to do. If someone told Deirdre what to do you'd almost be guaranteed she'd do the opposite, just to show she could. She had – she had spirit, you know? That isn't to say . . . I mean she believed passionately

147

in the Civil Rights, and I did too, sort of, and – and things were different then. Just for a couple of years. Sixty-eight and sixty-nine. It sounds like the worst kind of cliché now, but *then* . . . Things seemed possible, then. And after that party, we wrote to each other. Sometimes she'd phone me, your mammy, but she had to do it from a phone box because she didn't want anyone to know.

The phone box. The phone box at the bottom of our lane. I suddenly get a picture of my mother in my head, sneaking out and running down the lane to phone my daddy, her secret lover, her hair that reached down to her waist streaming out behind her.

—But we mostly wrote letters, my father is saying.

—Do you have any of them still?

—I don't know. I don't think so. Maybe.

—And then?

—And then, well, there were quite a few marches going on at the time and at first, we'd arrange to meet up after one of the marches. If I was off duty.

—And Mammy never told her family?

—About – about me? No, no. No, she did not. She most certainly did not. Them living in the Gaeltacht, me a wee Prod from up North, and a 'B' Special to boot – no, Deirdre said it was more than her life was worth for them to know. They didn't know about her going to the marches, either. She'd say she was going to stay with cousins up in Letterkenny. He pauses. But, you know, I've often wondered whether . . .

—Whether what, Da?

—Well. Whether it would have been such a big deal if she had've said to her parents. I never met them. By Deirdre's account they were old-fashioned and her father was a bit of a tyrant. But I think that when she – left, when she came up

North, it was her broke off contact with them rather than the other way round. My own mother, your nan, she thought I was off my bap at first, when I told her about Deirdre. She said I was courting trouble, I think were her words. But when she met Deirdre she liked her well enough, and there was never a question about Deirdre not being part of the family.

—I don't remember Nan.

—She passed away when you were only wee. But we used to visit her on Sunday afternoons. She lived in a wee cottage on the edge of the Lough. Used to take you out to play on the strand. And if I was working, you know, your mammy would take you by herself.

—Really?

—Aye. There was never any – acrimony. And I know there's bad blood between your aunty and me, and that's . . . He shakes his head.

—Go on.

—No, just as I say, I think Deirdre's family would have come round, if she'd given them the chance— He breaks off suddenly. Jesus, love, it's funny to be telling you this.

—No, don't stop! I need to know! Tell me what happened next. Like when did you and Mammy decide to get married?

My father looks away.

—Things had started to get bad in the autumn of nineteen seventy. The Troubles, I mean. Sixty-eight, sixty-nine, there was a lot of . . . Well, as I say, things were possible then in a way that a year or so later, they weren't. By then we'd been seeing each other – or not – off and on for two years, or thereabouts, but it became . . . less and less possible, shall we say, for a – a girl like Deirdre, and a fella like myself, to keep on meeting up. And I was thinking about joining the RUC proper by that stage. So we, ah, we decided to, to – well.

—To get married, you mean?

He tilts his head to one side and tugs at his beard.

—And when did Mammy go to Belfast?

—Let's see, now. It woulda been . . . He's looking at me funny. Deirdre came up to Belfast in the Easter of the following year. That's when we got married, he finishes in a rush.

—Oh.

My father spears some vegetables with his fork and then he puts the fork down and he pushes his plate to one side as well. Then he starts pulling at that beard of his again, hard, like he does when he's trying to think how to say something or when something's wrong.

He goes to say something, but as he coughs, music starts up in the corner of the restaurant, three fiddlers and a tin whistle, and he falls silent. There is a roar of appreciation and a great clatter of foot-stamping from the other customers. Normally we'd sit and listen for a bit, me bored out of my skull while my father joined in and made a fool out of himself; he's always been a right one for the auld tunes. Every time he comes down South he takes me out to some restaurant or lounge that's got traditional music on. Like it's his guilty pleasure. But now, when the music starts, he looks up, frowning.

—It's a wee bit noisy, isn't it, he says, and his voice is hoarse.

My father nods at the waiter for the bill. He's an old man, the waiter, with a scrubbed red face and curly white hair. He comes over and smacks his hands down on the table.

—And was everything all right for yez, was it?

—It was, aye.

—Grand, grand. And you'll be wanting coffee, will yez?

—No, you're all right.

—What about a bite of dessert for the young lady? He winks at me.

—In actual fact I think we're about ready to head on, my father goes.

—You'd not stay for the songs? Pity to leave, when they're just getting started.

—Another time maybe.

The waiter shrugs.

—Suit yourselves.

My father goes to get up and suddenly I panic: I've found out nothing concrete, and if I don't do it now I might not get another chance.

—When Mammy went across the water, I go.

My father starts, and looks at me sharply, and then looks away just as quickly.

—Da? I go.

He sinks back down into his seat. I'm watching his face carefully. Something runs through it, under the skin, some brief and strange change of expression.

—Right, he goes. When she – Right, right. Across the water, right. Then he mutters something, about he's not sure of his place and how he'll have to have a word with my aunty.

And then it hits me.

—You know, don't you? You know where she went! You *know*! I have jumped to my feet and I am almost shrieking and I am vaguely aware of people turning to look at us but I don't care. You do, don't you? You know and you're hiding it from me!

—*Saoirse*, he says, fiercely, grabbing my arm.

—Get off me! I yell.

—Get a grip! he says in a hoarse voice.

Flecks of his spittle land on my face and I jerk away but he's got a tight grip of my arm across the table and he twists me back round to face him again.

—Your mammy went across the water, he says, urgently.

151

And that's – that's – She went across the water and that's all we know, he finishes in a rush.

—I don't believe you! I go, and I don't know how, but somehow I know he's lying. You know something, I go. You and Aunt Bernadette both. You know something that you're not telling me.

And then all of a sudden I can't breathe. My mother is dead. *My mother is dead*. In the space of a second, I know it as clearly as if my father has just said the words.

—How did she— My whole body has gone to ice. Was it—

—Saoirse? he goes, and his voice sounds very far away. Vaguely, I feel him shaking my arm.

He is speaking, but there is a rushing in my ears and for a minute or so all I can hear is the sound of his voice booming and then receding.

—She's dead, isn't she, I finally manage to whisper.

—*What?* He stares at me, and then he laughs; a short, sharp guttural bark. No, Jesus, no; no, she's not – she's not dead, of course she's not—

I close my eyes. I feel weak and watery and far away. In the space of a few seconds my mother has died and been resurrected but in the end she's still as lost to me as she ever was.

—Come on, love, my father goes. Let's go.

Out in the car, we sit for a while without turning the engine on. You can hear snatches of music and laughter coming from the restaurant.

—This is hardly an ideal time but – well. You know the way I said there was something I wanted to ask you? my father says, abruptly.

—You what?

—Do you not remember I said there was something I wanted to ask you? he goes, impatiently.

—Yeah?

—Well, as I say this is hardly an ideal time, but . . . He clears his throat, and frowns.

—Da?

—We wondered if you'd like to spend the summer with us in Belfast, he goes in a rush.

The summer? *The summer?*

—The summer?

—Aye, well, you know, you'd come down after the Twelfth, when things quieten down a bit.

Why on earth would I want to spend the whole summer in *Belfast?*

—The summer's the busiest time here, Da, I can't leave my aunty and uncle.

—Well, love, I've already mentioned it to them and they say—

—Jesus, great! I explode. So youse've it all arranged behind my back, have youse?

—Ach, love, of course not. I only brought it up so's you wouldn't feel guilty if you did want to come.

—Thanks, that's awful considerate of you.

—Saoirse.

I've never been back to Belfast since we left, not once, and I've never met his – his *fancy woman*, and why would I want to now?

—Da, I go, not looking at him, Da, if you'd've wanted me to be with you in Belfast why didn't you want me all those years ago then?

He doesn't say anything. And suddenly I'm furious at him, slumped there like he's crumpled up inside, with his greying beard and the baldy patch at the back of his head; he's a sorry auld man, a sorry auld pathetic auld man, and he's not brave or dashing or, or *romantic*, he's a coward who couldn't make his marriage work and who gave up when things got bad, just gave up and didn't even try and fight, just hung his head and let things happen to him.

—*Say something*, I go, through gritted teeth, and he looks up at me with sad, droopy eyes, and as suddenly as it came, the rush of rage is gone, and I just feel weak; faraway and weak. Did you really come all this way, Da, to ask me if I wanted to come to Belfast? Because the thing is I really don't think I can, even if Aunt Bernadette and Uncle Brendan say it's all right, because they do need me in the summer, you know, and the thing is, why the whole summer, like, when I've never even been up for a weekend?

—Well, Saoirse, the reason is, what I wanted to say to you, is that Pauline and I are . . . Well, there's no way to say it, so I suppose I'd better just – well. We're going to have a baby, is the thing.

—You're what? Jesus Christ, you're *what*?

—Aye. She's just under two months to go. We didn't – I didn't say anything because, you see, she's miscarried, twice, over the past few years, but it's well into the third whatchamacallit now.

—You're having a *baby*?

—Aye. He's smiling, despite himself. A wee babby. Then he goes all serious again. It'll be born the end of July, so it will. And Pauline would really appreciate an extra pair of hands around, you know?

—My arse she would. I've never even met the woman!

—Well exactly, and wouldn't this be a good time to change all that? This wee babby's going to be your sister, Saoirse.

My sister. My sister?

—So . . . so it's a girl, then, I go.

I don't care. I don't care what it is. It's nothing to do with me.

—Aye. It's a girl. We haven't told people yet, you know? But she's a girl.

He's watching me, carefully. I make my face blank. Does This Look Like the Face of Someone Who Gives a Flying Fuck?

—We haven't thought of names, yet.

I don't say anything.

—We wondered what you thought. Your sister, you know?

And suddenly, there it is between us, like a ghost.

I am the first to speak. I say, It's been almost ten years, Dad.

He doesn't say anything for a bit.

—Ten years, I go, again.

—Aye, I know, he goes.

—Ten years this year. Do you ever think that?

—Do you think a day goes by when I don't think about how many bloody years it is?

He slams his fist against the steering wheel. His face is all twisted up. I've never seen him so – so angry before, so angry; and I don't know what to do. I don't say anything. I don't move. I think that if I move or if I say anything I'll start crying and then I won't be able to stop.

Then he goes, Sorry, pet.

—It's OK. I'm staring straight ahead out of the windscreen, trying to focus on one of the bricks in the wall in front, trying not to blink.

—No, it isn't OK, I'm sorry, you hear?

—I heard you. It's OK.

—I'm really sorry.

—I said it was OK.

—I didn't mean to snap like that.

—Really. Then I go, Can we go now, please? I want to go back home. Can we go?

I yank at my seatbelt and shove it in. My father sighs a shuddering sigh that seems to come from the deepest place inside of him, and he turns on the engine.

We don't say anything the whole way back. As my father drops me off at the bottom of the lane, he goes, You will still think about it, won't you? Coming to Belfast, I mean.

My throat closes over. How dare he?

He adds, quickly, And if you're still interested in your family history, on my side anyways, we can – I can take you round Greyabbey and all, where I grew up. That's where my side of the family's always come from.

And then he goes, And Saoirse, I did want you, all those years ago, I did want you so badly but—

—Fuck away off, I mutter, under my breath, but loud enough that he can hear, and I slam the door as hard as I can and bolt up the lane before he can say anything else or call me back.

When I get back, I ring Johnny's house from the hall phone, something I hardly ever do. For once, he's in.

—Johnny, I go, and suddenly I feel like I'm about to start gurning down the phone just at the sound of a friendly voice.

—Sha? Is that you, Sha?

—Yes, it's me, I go in a small voice.

—Can you speak up a bit? I can't hear ya.

—Johnny?

—Is everything OK there?

—Can we go on a drive? On one of our drives?

—What, now?

156

—Yes. Now.

—Aw, Sha, I can't. Not tonight. I've been . . . Me mam's worried, like. About the final couple of exams. She's got her eye on me. I can't get out of the house tonight.

—Oh.

There is a pause. I twist my fingers up in the coiled flex.

—Sha, are you there still? I think it's a bad line, I can't hear you.

—Yeah, no, I'm here. Johnny?

—Yeah?

—Will you, I mean, it's the Ball next week. I've been meaning to say. Will you—

—Yeah, it'll be good craic.

—You'll go with me?

—Course. Sha, I have to go now.

—OK. OK.

—See you soon, yeah?

—Yeah. Bye bye.

He's hung up. I put the phone back in its cradle and stand there for a second.

Johnny Mahon is my date for the Ball. But my father is having a baby, and I've never felt lonelier.

I don't tell anyone, not even my aunty or my uncle, about my father, and the baby, and Belfast. Do I want to spend the summer in Belfast indeed. The cheek of the man, I say to myself: the cheek of him.

My aunty asks, off-handedly, if I have any plans for the summer. I tell her that I'll help her like I always do. Any other plans? she presses, and I say, Practising my driving, and then I launch into how there's this new bar opened in Donegal Town that's putting on live music every weekend and how

Mairead and a couple of others want to drive up there and check out the bands. She narrows her eyes at me but she doesn't say anything else, and she doesn't mention my father, or spending the summer in Belfast. A couple of evenings later, my uncle asks if I'm not looking for a change of scene this summer. No, I say, firmly. The summer's fine the way it always is.

17

One evening, a few days before the end of term, Mairead comes clattering in through the back door. I hear the commotion from my room, and run down, two stairs at a time. Mairead is red-faced and out of breath.

—Is something the matter, Mairead? asks my aunt, sharply.

Mairead shakes her head.

—I just need to talk to Saoirse, she says.

—What's going on? says my aunty, frowning. She turns to me: Saoirse?

I shake my head. I have no idea.

—Leave them be, says my uncle. No doubt it's girl-talk about this Ball of theirs, ey Mairead?

She smiles, weakly, and we hurry up to my room.

Before I have a chance even to ask her the words are tumbling out of her.

—*What?* I go, and she needs to repeat it all before it starts to sink in.

Johnny and Éamon Mahon have been arrested for possession of firearms and on two counts of suspected paramilitary involvement. They, and two older men from down the coast, were under surveillance, and proof enough to arrest the four of them came when weapons and other suspicious items including ammonium nitrate were found with their fingerprints in a disused barn on the Dennehy farm. It's the biggest news since the massive arms dump was uncovered at Malin

Head earlier on in the year, and the *gardaí* claimed they'd smashed a major paramilitary ring.

—The Mahons' uncle, Mairead goes, breathlessly, you know he's in jail for being in the Provos? And Johnny's most likely going to go to jail, too, she goes. 'Cause he's eighteen now, isn't he? He's an adult. He's in deep fecking shit now.

Earlier on this evening, she says, Johnny's mam came tearing up the road to Mairead's house to ask her cousin's family for help with the bail for her two boys.

—She's still there, Mairead goes. My da's gone down the station with John Mahon Senior and my mam and Úna Mahon and a few others are in the kitchen making phone calls and crying and Jaysus it's hectic in there. I slipped away because I had to come and tell you, in case you hadn't heard yet, before it got properly out.

She stops, all of a sudden.

—Did you – you didn't *know*, did you? Is that what you've been acting all funny about? Did you know? Were you part of it, too?

—No, I go, *no*!

But . . .

—But that's why *he* was acting so funny, I go, half to myself.

—He was acting funny? *Was* he? Like how? goes Mairead, eagerly.

—Just . . . just distracted.

—I asked you were things OK with Johnny!

—Yeah . . .

—I did! I asked you and all! she crows.

—Poor Johnny!

—Stupid Johnny, more like. Getting mixed up in the likes of that. Probably did it for the excitement, didn't he? For the glamour. Secret trips and guns and all. Like playing soldiers, only for real. That's what his mam said to my mam. She said he was a silly boy entangled in something he didn't understand. Going along with his older brother. She said she was furious at Éamon, that Éamon should've known better for himself, let alone for leading his wee brother astray. But she said Johnny was always easily led and out for a quick thrill. But saying that's no use now. He's an adult, in the eyes of the law.

—Oh Jesus.

—What? What, what is it?

Another thing has just occurred to me: my aunt and uncle. What – oh, Jesus – what will they think?

—My aunt and uncle, I whisper.

—What about them?

—They don't know.

—They'll know soon enough. Everyone'll know soon enough.

—No, they don't know about Johnny. About me and Johnny.

—They don't *know*?

—No. They haven't a clue that I've been seeing him. My aunty says they're a bad lot, the Mahons. 'Cause of their uncle, I think. She doesn't hold with politics, my aunty.

We stare at each other.

—She's going to kill you, your aunty, Mairead goes. If she finds out. Then she adds, Hey, but she might not find out. If you really don't have anything to do with it—

—I *don't*!

—Well, then, you won't be involved.

—But Johnny! I have to go and see Johnny!

—I don't think you'll be able to.

—I have to! I have to find a way to see him. I have to ask him if it's true. Maybe he's just got mixed up by mistake.

But I know even as I say it that's not true.

—What shall I do, Mairead?

—I don't know, she goes.

And then it's too late to do anything.

My uncle calls me down the stairs.

—Saoirse, he calls, in a strained voice. There's a *garda* here to see you.

The *garda* is standing in the kitchen with my aunt and uncle, both of whom are white as sheets. They stare at me when I come into the room.

—Mairead, says my uncle, I think you'd better be going.

She nods, wide-eyed. Then she reaches out and grabs my hand and squeezes it and mouths, I'm sorry, before turning and going through the door that my uncle's holding open for her.

The *garda* is a friend of Michael Deegan, he says, and he says he's here unofficially. We sit in the living room, my aunt perched on the edge of the settee, the *garda* in the good armchair, Uncle Brendan's armchair, and my uncle in the hard-backed chair in the corner. I sit on the footrest of the sofa, facing the semi-circle they make, like I'm on trial or something, and it hits me: I am, sort of. Oh Jesus.

—You have a hell of a lot of explaining to do, my aunt begins.

—Bernadette, murmurs my uncle.

She flares up at him: No! You're not going to tell me to go easy on her this time, Brendan. This is serious.

—I didn't know anything about it, honest! I burst. I knew nothing, nothing at all!

The deserted barn, and the men coming out of it.

—Honest to God I didn't!

I should have guessed. How could I not have realized? Or, a tiny wee voice says, or was it that you didn't want to know?

—You knew nothing at all? says the *garda*. And did you not guess anything? Were there no hints, no odd behaviour, nothing like that?

I look at him, and bite my lip. What good will saying anything now do? But, on the other hand, does holding my tongue make me guilty?

—I . . . I start to speak, but my mouth is dry. I swallow. I—

—Saoirse's a good girl, my aunty interjects, her lips pressed tightly together. At least . . . she adds, coldly, the Saoirse I know.

And then the *garda* says, It's all right. I didn't think that young Saoirse here was messed up in anything of the sort. As I said, this is an informal visit, just to fill you in, because it'll be all over the papers tomorrow. He hesitates. And to say, be careful of the company you keep, colleen. Your name was brought up at the station, and we asked your Mr Mahon about you, and do you know what he said?

I shake my head, slowly. What did he say? Jesus, what did Johnny say?

—He said, and I'm sorry to repeat this, he said: 'I needed an excuse for if I was seen around auld Dennehy's farm. And as a bonus who'd suspect anything of the daughter of an RUC man?'

I gape at him.

Johnny needed an *excuse*? And my being known as the daughter of an RUC man was a *bonus*?

—*What?*

—I'm sorry, miss.

Bridget: Why'd he want to ask you out? Sure you've never even spoken to him before, have you?

The *garda* gets to his feet, and puts his cap on.

—Thank you for coming over, my uncle says, standing up as well.

—Not at all, says the *garda*. Any friend of Michael's. Then he adds, If there's any trouble – there shouldn't be – but if there is, just give me a ring at the station.

—That's very kind of you, says Aunt Bernadette.

—Not at all, says the *garda*, again.

—Thanking you for your time and trouble, she says.

My aunty cries. I can't remember ever seeing her cry before. Her crying makes me cry, too. I thought she'd be furious at me, but she's not; or at least, she's more sad than furious, which is worse.

It's way past midnight by the time we've talked over everything, and I've confessed and explained, again and again, how Johnny would drive me home from school and sometimes we'd go to the cinema and that, and I didn't want to tell them because I knew they wouldn't approve of me having a boyfriend let alone one of the Mahons who my aunty had made it quite clear she didn't approve of. It all sounds so stupid, now.

In the end, they decide that I'm grounded for the whole of the summer, and I should thank my lucky stars it's not worse, my uncle tells me. I'm allowed to go to the school Ball, but that's to be the only exception – and for a while my aunty didn't even think I should go to that, only I've already got the dress and what have you. But I don't even want to go to that any more, not now I haven't got a date, not now I've been so – *humiliated*, because everyone will know, soon enough, that Johnny Mahon was using me as a convenient excuse, that he didn't really like me anyways. I'm not sure which is worse: the knowing that, or the fact that everyone else will know.

—Who'd've thought it, my aunty says, over and over again. I'm just an ordinary person, she says, trying to live an ordinary life.

She says: Is there no escape from it all? Is there no escape?

18

Finally, it's the last day of school, and the day of the Summer Ball. We get out at midday. The others are going for lunch in a pub in Glenties, and then to get their hair and make-up done, but I say that my aunty wants me back home. It's not true – I haven't told her that we get a half-day today – but I need to be by myself; the others have been tiptoeing around me as if I'm an invalid, or there's something wrong with me, and I can't summon up the energy to take part in their gossipy banter about the Ball.

—I'll do your hair for you this evening, goes Bridget, taking my arm. She's been being specially nice to me since it all came out about Johnny and Éamon Mahon. You could do loads with your hair. So long and that. I'll think of something good. It'll look gorgeous, Sha.

—Yeah and Aoife's sister can do your eye make-up, chips in Mairead. Can't she, Aoife?

—Yeah! Aoife nods, enthusiastically. Aoife's sister's at college, learning to be a beautician.

—We're going to have a grand auld time, Mairead goes.

—Yeah, I go, trying to sound grateful, and I am, sort of, grateful that they're all being so nice to me: but all I can think of is what a fool Johnny made out of me, and how disappointed in me my aunty is. I wonder if she regrets taking me in all those years ago, and the thought aches like a deep bruise in my chest.

*

I don't want to go back to Gweebarra Sands, but I don't know where else to go. Then it occurs to me that it's as good a time as any to do what I've been meaning to do for a while: visit the Public Records Office. This is because there's something that's been nagging at me: the way that, when I asked my father if my mother was dead, he laughed in that incredulous way, in a way that said, *Don't be ridiculous*. She's not dead, of course she's not, he said. And the more I think about it, the more I think there was something not quite right in the way he said it; something guilty, as if he wasn't telling the truth. I don't know anything about how deaths are registered and recorded, but I reason that I may as well try the area Public Records Office, just in case. If there isn't a death certificate, I'm no worse off than before, and if there is, then at least, finally, I'll *know*.

I'd imagined that I'd have to spend the whole afternoon hoking through big auld books of parish records or what have you, especially considering I don't even know the years I'm after or anything. But everything's on computer, and all I have to do is tell the lady the surname I'm looking for and the lists of names and dates flash up on the screen in only a few seconds. There are lots of O'Conors, and the lady scrolls down until I see Deirdre O'Conor, my mother.

—There, I go. That's her. That's – her. That's who I'm looking for.

Only a couple of minutes later I've found Aunt Bernadette, and her parents, my mother's parents – my grandparents, I think with a start – and *their* parents, even. There're loads of O'Conors registered at Gweebarra Parish Church.

—Well, you certainly belong here, the lady goes.

—Me? I go. I'm not an O'Conor. I mean my name. But yeah, maybe. Yeah.

I don't really know what to say to that.

—I can print out copies of the certificates for you, the lady goes. Which ones in particular is it you're after?

—Can I have them all? I mean, everything for the O'Conors in Gweebarra Parish for, like . . . the last fifty years?

—Certainly. It won't take a minute. The lady smiles at me. Dead easy, isn't it?

—Yeah, I go. I didn't – I didn't expect – I mean, I didn't think it would be so easy, I stutter. To find them.

—Well, looks like you've found what you're looking for.

—Yeah, I go, nodding like a fool. Yeah.

I take the certificates over to a table by the window and spread them out.

The first two pieces of paper are death certificates.

My mother's father, Seamus O'Conor, died in December 1977, and the cause of death is given as: Stroke.

My mother's mother, Cathleen O'Conor, died only a few weeks afterwards, in February 1978, and the cause of death is given as: Heart Failure.

I would've been six then. Six-and-a-half. I try to think back to then: Christmas, it would have been; I try to think what I would have been doing, what my mother would have been doing, when her parents, my grandparents that I'd never met, died; but I can't remember anything. Mammy never talked about her family, or where she was from. The first I ever heard of Gweebarra Bay was when we were on our way here to live, and I remember asking loads of questions about my brand-new aunty and uncle and my mother losing her patience and snapping: I've been dead to them for years. It's strange the little things you remember. I remember that because I remember thinking how funny it was, how they must've thought Mammy was dead but now there she was,

168

come back to life to surprise them. Then it strikes me: I wonder if my mother even knew that her parents had died. Surely if she'd known she would've gone to the funerals, and I don't remember a time when she left us, ever. And I overheard my aunty say, once, how before she got the phone call out of the blue saying my mother and me were coming to Gweebarra Bay, she didn't even know that I existed. I feel odd remembering that. As if part of me's gone transparent. A shiver goes down my spine and I shake it off and pick up the next piece of paper in my little pile.

This third sheet is my aunty's birth certificate: Bernadette Cathleen O'Conor was born in 1937. There are two more birth certificates, and two death certificates: a boy, Seamus Patrick, born in 1939, and a girl, Mary Patricia, born in 1943. Both of them died when they were less than a year old, and the cause of death is given in each case as: Sudden & Unexpected.

My aunty's never once mentioned that she had a wee brother and sister who died. She would've been two, and then six. Jesus.

There's no death certificate for my mother: the final piece of paper is her birth certificate. Deirdre Mary O'Conor, born in May 1951. May 1951: a gap of seven and a bit years between wee Mary Patricia dying and my mother being born. It hits me: she must've been very young when she married my father. And then something else occurs to me.

I work out the dates in my head, and then I do the figures again on a piece of paper, just to be sure. No wonder my father was ill at ease when I was asking him questions. It's glaringly obvious: how could I not have realized at the time?

My mother was born in 1951. That means that when she met my father in the Civil Rights March in August 1968, she was only seventeen, barely any older than I am now. He said she was young but I didn't know she was that young. And they got married in the Easter of 1971. But I was born at the end of August of the same year, which is less than five months later. So there we have it. I must've been – conceived – in the December, it would be, of 1970: that Easter, when my mother, not yet twenty, left her family and came up to Belfast, she was already over five months pregnant with me. I never thought; I never even suspected: I was her accident; her disgrace; I was the reason she had to leave in the first place.

I'm still sitting at the table when the lady comes over and asks if there's anything else she can help me with.

—No, I say, emptily. No thank you.

She tells me sorry, but they're closing in five minutes.

—It's all right, I say. I don't need to know any more.

—Is it a history project you're working on?

—Sort of, yeah, I go.

—We're open on Saturdays until midday if you need to come back.

—No thank you, I go. I've found out everything I needed to know.

I gather up the sheaf of papers and fold them carefully into my bag.

Aunt Bernadette is hanging out washing in the garden when I get back to Gweebarra Sands. She's got her back to me. I take a few steps across the grass, and stop. A couple of blocks of peat have tumbled down off the pile, and I pick them up and stack them back in place. Then I go, Aunt Bernadette?

Bernadette Cathleen née O'Conor, born in 1937, turns round with a start.

—Oh! she goes. You put the heart crossways in us there, you did! She turns back to her washing. Give us a hand, love?

I stay where I am.

—You're late back, she goes. Where did you get to?

—Aunty, I go.

—Yes, love? she says, absently. She puts a couple of clothes pegs in her mouth and tussles with the shirt that's flapping in her face.

—I found out about my mother, I go.

—What's that? my aunty says through the clothes pegs in her mouth.

—I said, I found out about my mother.

She turns slowly to face me, clutching the bundle of damp clothes she's holding tight to her chest.

—You what?

—I found it out, I go, again.

Her arms open in slow motion and the clothes tumble to the ground.

—Oh, Saoirse. Dear God, Saoirse. However did you—

—Why didn't you tell me?

—Oh, *céadsearc*, I—

We stare at each other.

—Why didn't you tell me, I repeat, thickly, and then I go, Was I the reason?

She takes a step towards me, stepping over the clothes getting all muddy on the ground, then stops.

—Saoirse, she goes.

—You've hidden it from me. All these years you've hidden it from me.

—Saoirse, she goes, again. Let me explain.

And then she tells me.

It is my uncle who comes down to the beach to find me. I don't know how long I've been there, just standing, facing the sea, letting the wind whip my hair about and snatch the water from my eyes. The only thing I can think of is how, when my mother disappeared, I'd spend hours and hours on this beach. It's a thin strip of flat white sand, three-quarters of a mile or so long, with rocky outcrops at each end, and nothing to shelter it from the vastness of the Atlantic Ocean. No one ever comes to this beach. You can't surf here because of the rocks, and there are better beaches, bigger beaches, down the coast, and on the other side of the town; beaches where you can swim safely, or sit in the lee of the wind. But I used to love the emptiness of my beach, and the way that, if the wind was strong enough, I could face the sea and run and run as hard as I could and the wind would be pushing against me and almost lifting me up so it felt like I was flying.

My uncle rests one hand on my shoulder, but he doesn't say anything, and we stand side by side, looking out at the sea. The tide is out, about as far out as it goes. Beyond the frothy white breakers the waters are grey and choppy, occasionally glinting with silver when the faint light breaks through the thin layer of cloud.

After a while, he says, You're shivering. Shall we go back in?

I don't know. I don't know what to do. I hadn't noticed I was cold.

—Your aunty loves you more than anything, he goes. And then he goes, We never meant to hurt you.

I stare at him blankly.

—Shall we go back? he says, again, and mutely, I nod.

—It was your Ball this evening, wasn't it, he says.

—I can't go now, I whisper.

—No, he says. No.

Then he says, I'm sorry, love.

He takes my arm gently, and we walk back up the beach and to the house.

—When can I go there? I say. When can I – visit?
Aunt Bernadette looks at me, and looks away.
—I'll phone, she says.
—But when?
Her face is in her hands.
—Please, Saoirse, love, please just—
—No, I interrupt. No.
—Sunday, perhaps, she says, without lifting her head.
—This coming Sunday.
—This coming Sunday.
—You'd better phone now, then.
And then I turn and walk away.

The night before, I don't sleep; the whole night I lie there, drifting, and it's like I'm drifting at a hundred miles an hour and I can't for the life of me get properly to sleep.

I keep remembering a memory I didn't realize I had, a memory of a summer's day; and in the memory it's hot, which is what makes me realize that I must have made the memory up, because everyone knows that in Belfast it rains all the time, that Belfast is never hot. But in this made-up memory it's hot, broilingly hot, and Mammy is lying outside, somewhere, she's lying outside telling Daisy and me stories and threading daisies into chains to make necklaces out of. I rack my mind for more details, because what I'm seeing is just like a brief snapshot, but in the long suspended moments just before dawn, as I try desperately to get back into the memory, the memory slides into a nightmare; I suddenly feel cold all over and out of the corner of my eye I am sure I can see these long spindly ghostly fingers flexing and feeling and reaching out for my ankles, trying to get a hold of me and pull me under the earth, through the tree roots and into the kingdom of the dead.

I sit up with a jolt, and it's the sheets my legs are tangled around. I kick them away from me, and lie back down, and it feels silly, but I cross my arms across my chest and lie there like one of the old saints, as Aunt Bernadette taught me to when I first arrived, in case Jesus and the angels came for me in the night, so I would be ready.

When morning comes, finally, with the grey watery light seeping in the skylight, I am so tired that I feel translucent. I stagger over to my little sink and cup my hands under the tap and splash cold water on my face until my skin tightens so much it feels like it's about to break and I am gasping out loud, but I still don't feel any more real.

It was my fault, you see. Why Daisy died; and then, why Mammy left. I've carried it inside of me always, that knowledge, like a smooth cold pebble in my chest that makes me not able to breathe properly; and now, added to it, is the discovery that it was because of me, too, because she was pregnant with me, that Mammy left her family and home in the first place. Why Mammy left; why Daisy died; why Mammy left, again. All of it, all of it: it was all me.

19

La Retraite, the house is called, and it is set back from the road, enclosed by a high wall of neat rust-coloured bricks. After my uncle has left me off, he turns the car at the bottom of the road, and drives away, and I watch him; I watch until he has gone, and when the car has disappeared, I walk up to the gates. They are smooth iron, cool to the touch (and the touch of iron keeps the fairies away, a voice says in my head), and I push down the curved handle and lean against the bars and the gate swings slowly, heavily open. The house is made of grey stone, four storeys high, and it is built in a slight rise, with a flight of steps to the front door, and six slim colonnades supporting the porch. There are two enormous bay windows each side of the porch, and they glitter blankly where the afternoon sun catches them, like big blind eyes, I think with a shiver. Then I tell myself: Catch yourself on, Saoirse, get a grip! This isn't a fairy story. And then, when I look again, the windows just look like windows. It must have been a grand house, once; it must have been a powerful rich family lived here. I count the windows, and then, mid-twenties, stop, confused: I have a hazy memory of counting other windows on another big house on another hill. I shake my head to shake the daydream away. Come on, I tell myself, you're letting your imagination run away with you. Get a grip! I say again, this time aloud. My voice sounds thin and weedy. I'm still holding the gate open. I let go, and it clanks shut behind me. Everything is quiet; the house sits, big and square and solid-looking, presiding over its long sloping lawns and raked path and tidy flower beds. The brim of my new velvet hat keeps flopping in my eyes. Stupid bloody hat. I pull it off and stuff it into my bag. Then I straighten out the pleats of my skirt. The woollen waistband is making me itch. But seeing as how smart the house looks, I'm glad I wore the skirt instead of leggings or jeans and trainers; Aunt Bernadette was right. My feet in their clompy patent heels scrunch all the way up the gravel drive. Each dusty crunch scuffs the toes that Uncle Brendan shined so carefully for me. I clip-clop up the shallow stone steps, and press the big brass button to ring the bell. I can hear a muffled echo of the clanging. I wipe my damp hands on the back of my skirt. No one comes. I go to ring again. But as I lift my hand, the door suddenly opens inwards, and a nun appears, smiling.

—Good afternoon, my child, are you—

—I'm Saoirse Pentland, I say at the same time, Saoirse O'Conor Pentland that is, and I'm here to – and my voice is high and girlish – and I'm here to, to see my—

—Yes, she smiles. You're here to see Deirdre.

—Yes, I say, Deirdre, I'm here to see Deirdre O'Conor. Pentland. Deirdre.

—I'm Sister Mary Aloysius, she says.

—Pleased to meet you, Sister, I mumble. My tongue feels too big for my mouth, all swollen and dry.

—Well, come in, she goes, taking a step backwards and opening the door wider.

I step up to the threshold.

—This is the reception area, she goes, gesturing gracefully around her. If you'd just like to take a seat here for a moment? They're finishing off their lunch.

—Oh, oh, lunch, of course, I say, foolishly, as if I should have known.

—Have a seat, she goes again, indicating a red velvet sofa under one of the bay windows, and she turns to leave. But at the double doors she pauses, and she turns back again, and takes a step towards me, and says, slowly, Your mother, Deirdre—

She breaks off, and pauses.

—Your mother, Deirdre, has had a hard time of it, you'll understand, and she'll maybe not care to remember things. She speaks as if she's choosing each and every word with great care. A lot of our ladies have had terrible traumas in their pasts, and it's in the peacefulness we have here that they find a degree of redemption. You do understand?

—Yes, I nod, and I keep on nodding even when she's turned away to leave the room.

Redemption?

I stand for a minute, staring at a vase of flowers that someone's placed on the little circular table beside the door. The china vase is sitting in the exact middle of the table, and the flowers are arranged just so, perfectly spaced between long green droopy strands of fern. I stare at those perfect flowers. I have the sudden urge to tweak one of them, or move the vase ever so slightly to one side. Get a grip! I tell myself, for the third time today, and I dig my nails into the palms of my hands and look around the rest of the room. It's done up in wood panelling that's stained the colour of walnut, and still-life paintings of bowls of fruit are hung on the walls in elaborate gilded frames. It's a gloomy room, despite having the two big windows. The dark walls absorb all of the light until there's barely enough left to see by. I shiver, and sit down on the sofa. It sags in the middle, and

I shuffle forwards and perch carefully on the edge. The material of the sofa is worn thin in places, and the arms have tight shiny patches along their tops. There's a faint smell of polish and dust in this room, together with a touch of canteen food, like the thin smell of boiled fish. I turn around to look out of the bay window behind me. To the left, there is a glen, and just about visible through the trees is a stream that bubbles and spills downwards in choppy little waterfalls; to the right, to the west, you can see the hazy shadows of the Blue Stack Mountains, wee smudges on the skyline.

—Saoirse?

I whip round and almost lose my balance. It's Sister Mary Aloysius, alone.

—Deirdre will be down shortly. Would you care to take a cup of tea and a biscuit?

—No thank you! I bleat.

—Why don't I have a seat beside you, then, and I'll tell you a little bit about the history of this house while we wait.

She draws a straight-backed wooden chair up to the sofa, and sits down with her hands folded neatly in her lap. I wriggle to sit upright on the sofa, and it creaks loudly.

She smiles at me. I can feel my cheeks burning. I try and look ladylike and smile back.

The house has a southerly aspect, she tells me; positioned to catch the afternoon sun, it was built at a time when, if the weather was fine, a table with tea and bread and butter and slices of cake could be carried out down the steps to the grassy terrace, and the ladies could sit and talk, and the children and the dogs – for in those days there were always Irish wolfhounds, whose siblings and descendants could be recognized throughout all of Donegal – tumbled together on the

178

lawn. In those days, the house, known locally as the Big House, was called Mount Fitzpatrick, after the generations of the same family who had lived there since the eighteenth century, when the Planters moved beyond the Pale. That the grand Protestant house is now taken over by Catholic nuns, she says with an upwards twist of her mouth, is a fact that few people have cause to remark upon these days; those who remember the shootings and the great fire of the twenties, when most of the east wing and the coach houses burned down and the Fitzpatrick family fled to England, they were young then, those people, and they are old now, in their seventies or eighties, at least, and they have their own lives to occupy them in the long hours of remembering.

Her voice is clear as water, and she talks on, calmly, unhurriedly, inclining her head and smiling kindly at me, and I listen and nod, trying all the while to look polite and interested. Then she breaks off, and stands up, and I stand, too: another nun, younger and plumper, has come into the room, and behind her, it must be . . . behind her is my mother.

She takes a step forwards, and the double doors swing closed behind her and rock, slightly.

—*Saoirse*, she breathes, like a sigh; and then she says it again, and it's sharper this time: *Seer*-sha.

I go to speak but my throat has closed over.

—Well, says Sister Mary Aloysius. Here we are.

—Saoirse, she goes, again, and then she goes, It's me.

She is thin, and slightly stooped. Her hair is short, bobbed bluntly, and streaked with grey, and she has no make-up on. She is wearing a brown knee-length skirt and a loose navy cardigan over a fawny-coloured blouse, and she's holding a bright pink canvas bag patterned with swirling orange spirals. I can't help staring at that psychedelic bag.

—Are you going to say hello to your mother? Sister Mary Aloysius asks.

My mother. My mother who, all these past years, has been living less than two hours' drive from me; my mother who had *problems*; my mother who had some kind of breakdown, and disappeared one evening, and was found by Manus Dennehy, wandering barefoot in the fields by the Bay with hardly a stitch of clothing on her, and was bundled into the car and taken to hospital and then sent here, to La Retraite, to this place outside of where she's never since set foot.

I realize I'm standing there with my mouth open like I'm looking to catch flies, as my aunty would say. I close my mouth. The Sister touches me gently on the elbow, as if to propel me forwards. I feel myself swaying slightly.

I clear my throat.

—Hello, Mother, my voice says.

—Hello.

I adjust my bag where the strap's cutting into my shoulder. Then I remember to stand up straight and not slouch.

I clear my throat again.

Then the other nun, the one who brought my mother in, says, It's a nice afternoon for the garden, Deirdre, why don't you take Saoirse for a walk in the orchard and you can find somewhere quiet to sit and talk?

—Yes, why don't you? says Sister Mary Aloysius, and without waiting for an answer she sweeps forward across the polished floor towards the doors.

The four of us, then, the plump nun guiding my mother, Sister Mary Aloysius and I following behind like a school crocodile, walk down a wood-panelled corridor with pale yellow linoleum floors, and through another set of double doors, which lead to a hallway with high ceilings and a wide sweeping entrance, then through another door off the hallway into a big lounge, with wooden chairs and easy chairs and tables and bookshelves and an unwatched TV blaring out some family game show. The carpet in this room is brown, and the walls are pale orange. Glass patio doors open on to a wide garden, with gnarly old apple trees and benches dotted about. We pause on the broad step outside the patio.

—Here we are, says Sister Mary Aloysius, and she and the plump nun smile at me and my mother.

—This is where we spend our afternoons when we have the weather, says the plump nun, raising one hand and fanning her fingers outwards to the garden. We like to get some fresh air and sunlight, don't we, Deirdre?

The other inmates – Jesus, I can't call them *inmates*. What, then? Patients, occupants? And then I see a sign on the wall, 'Residents' Lounge'; residents, then, residents – the other *residents* are strolling around the lawn in groups of twos or threes, or digging at flower beds, or sitting reading or sewing.

—We have a nice life here for ourselves, says Sister Mary Aloysius.

—Yes, I say.

Then she says, brightly, We'll leave the two of you here, then, shall we? You can take Saoirse for a walk around the lake, Deirdre. I'm sure she'd like to see the swans. And you'll be back in good time for tea, won't you?

—Oh yes, Sister, my mother says, sounding for all the world like me or Mairead or Bridget agreeing with Sister Bonaventure that we'll have our Irish grammar learned for the next lesson.

—Off you go, then, and have a nice afternoon.

We walk through the garden in silence, and we sit down at the far end, at a circular bench built around one of the trees.

—You've turned out well, so you have, my mother says, abruptly.

—Have I?

—Aye, you have. You've turned out well. Bernadette's shown me photos, from time to time, but you look better than the photos.

—She's shown you – photos?

—Aye.

—Of me.

—I never forgot you, you know— She breaks off. Aye. Smart. You look smart.

We both gaze at my pleated skirt and my patent heels.

—Let me see you properly, now, she goes, suddenly. Sit up straight. She reaches out one finger and lightly touches the gold cross at my throat. You see . . . she goes, softly, and it's as if she's not speaking to me but to someone else, You see, I was right, you know. I was right.

I can't look at her any more. But I can feel the way she's looking at me; she's looking at me like she's asking for something.

—I knew that Belfast was no place for a wee girl to be growing up. I was right, wasn't I? Wasn't I right?

I can't speak.

—How old are you? she goes.

—Sixteen, I go. Then I add, Almost seventeen.

—Aye, she goes. You would be, wouldn't you?

—Yes, I say, stupidly.

Then she goes, You don't look how I'd imagined you.

—I don't?

—No, you don't.

I wait for her to say more, but she turns away, and so I go, How did you imagine me, then?

182

—Different.

—Different how?

—Just different, she goes. Then she goes, It's that you look grown up. I hadn't imagined you grown up.

Grown up? Do I look grown up?

—I've still another year of school left to do, I go.

—And what will you do after school?

—I don't know. I've been thinking, I'll maybe apply to do History at university.

—History?

—At UCD. Or maybe Trinity. If I get the grades.

—Trinity?

—Yeah. Dublin, you know?

—Aye. She nods once or twice, slowly. History, she goes.

—Yeah. Maybe. I don't know. The past and that, you know?

—Aye. There's enough of that to keep you going.

I don't know what to say when she says that.

—There's surely enough, she goes, again.

—Yeah, I say, feebly.

She doesn't say anything else and I think: this is it, this is my chance.

—Talking of the past, I go, but even as I'm saying it I cringe to hear myself saying it like that. I start again: There's a couple of things I'd like to ask you, about the past and that.

My mother turns sharply to look at me, her eyes narrowing.

—It doesn't do to be dredging up the past, she snaps. The past is past.

—I know, but the thing is, there're just a few things that I'd – that I'd . . . I stammer to a halt.

My mother stands up, and folds her arms across her chest. She presses her lips together. I notice a faint pattern of lines etched into her cheeks, and like a web around her mouth.

—You've your own life to be living, she says, a little more quietly. Live your own life and don't think about what's done and gone.

She turns her back to me. I stand up too, then.

—But I can't, I say to her back. I can't!

She gives a quick shrug of her shoulders.

—You have to, she says, still with her back to me, cold again.

I close my eyes. My mother, eyes dancing, laughing up at my father when he sang that she was *the Belle of Belfast City*. My mother, lying on the tartan rug in the garden and piercing daisy-stems with her thumbnail. The screeching explosion of a car bomb going off at the end of our street and the *whoompf* of flames that you could see through our bedroom window and my mother there, stroking our hair and saying, softly, Shh now, it's all right, nothing can happen to you so long as Mammy's here, Mammy won't let anything happen to you. Mammy tying my hair in a side ponytail so I could see the ends of the ribbon and Mammy showing me how to wind the ballerina box and Mammy letting me cuddle in bed with her on nights when Daddy was on lates. Walking past the mural of King Billy on his white horse on the way to Avoniel Leisure Centre and asking why can't we have paintings on our house and Mammy saying, Ach, now, you'll understand once you're a wee bit older, and me saying, But why, Mammy, and Mammy squeezing my hand and saying, Sha-sha, perhaps today's the day you'll swim without armbands, do you think you can, and me forgetting about the paintings on the houses and skipping along a bit faster to get to the swimming pool. Mammy reading us Cúchulainn, and telling us how Fand was the most beautiful woman you could ever imagine, and me smiling inside, knowing all the while that my mammy was more beautiful than Fand, even, for didn't my daddy say so. And then . . . and then Mammy, eyes all blank and staring, lying in the bed in the smallest guest room. Mammy barefoot in her old C&A nightie at the end of the lane, crying and twisting away and hitting out at Uncle Brendan as he yanked at her arm and then got her in a fireman's lift back to the kitchen of Gweebarra Sands, and my aunty shouting at me to get back to bed and what was I doing downstairs at this time of night. The car doors in the middle of the night, and the crunches and scuffles on the gravel driveway, and the footsteps on the landing and the guest-room door opening and closing and opening again and the draught and the sudden clattering and smashing and me too scared to open my eyes and in the morning five of the seashells shattered where in the rush and in the commotion of the comings and goings they'd been knocked to the floor. Then . . . then Mammy's clothes gone, and one of the suitcases gone, and the ballerina box, which had belonged to Mammy before it belonged to me, belonged to Mammy when she was my age, that, too, gone. Aunt Bernadette taking me on her squashy lap and stroking my hair, her breath in hot gulping gusts on the back of my neck, telling me that everything was all right, that everything was going to be all right, that I needed to go back to bed.

I open my eyes again. My mother hasn't moved; she's still got her back to me. After a bit, she says, without turning around, We can take a walk around the lake. Would you like to take a walk around the lake?

The lake is a large ornamental pond with a tidily raked gravel path around it. We walk halfway around, and then sit for a while on a wooden bench facing the house. Neither of us says anything. My mother sits straight-backed and still, with only an occasional tremor flickering across her face; she is chewing at the inside of her cheeks, I think, watching her sideways, and I remember how when she was cross with us she would suck in her cheeks and make an impatient, pouty movement with her lips. I look away. Carefully scattered water lilies float on the surface of the lake, and even the ducks seem neat and sedate. There are two swans gliding across the glassy water. Everything is just so. I think of the story of the king who didn't want his only child to know death or decay, and so employed hundreds upon hundreds of servants to remove every single withering leaf and wilting blade of grass from the gardens of the palace and for miles beyond. One of the swans suddenly plunges its neck underwater and its tail waggles in the air. For a second, its big black feet flap above the water. Then it rights itself and carries on its stately drift across the lake.

Daisy's favourite story was the Children of Lir, and there were times, at the beginning of my life in Gweebarra Bay, when I wondered if she had been turned into a swan, like Fionnuala and her brothers. In my book – Mammy's book – of Folk Tales and Legends, the wicked witch sneered, *Ye shall never be free until the woman from the south be united to the man from the north, and that shall not be for nine hundred years, and unto ye I shall grant only this: that ye may keep your own speech, and ye shall sing, and your song shall have the power to make fighting men lay down their arms.* Nine hundred years: when nine hundred years had passed, and St Patrick had come to the Isle of Birds, and McHowg came to the Isle of Birds and broke the enchantment, Fionnuala and her brothers held their human shapes for the slightest fraction of a second only, before their flesh turned to dust and they clattered down in front of the altar a heap of dry brown bones, Fionnuala's cry – of joy? Of relief? Of pain? – already a fading echo in the air.

—You see the swans? I say, and my mother looks at me and frowns, slightly. I didn't mean – I just meant . . .

But I don't know what I meant.

—You had to leave Gweebarra Bay because of me, I say, stumbling a bit as I say it. Didn't you? Because you were pregnant with me.

The words whip out of her mouth: I'd've gone anyway.

—That's not true.

—Don't you dare be telling me what is and what isn't true! I chose. I chose to go, you understand? I had my choice.

Then, Saoirse, she says, softer, after a bit, Saoirse, are you happy?

—Happy? Yes. Yes, I'm – happy.

—Good. It wasn't – Belfast wasn't – a happy place.

—But it was, I say, quickly, and the words are out of me before I have a chance to hear them in my head or even to know what I'm going to say. Daisy and I, it was happy, it was very happy, before. And you were happy, too, Mammy, I remember. Before.

My mother turns abruptly away.

—You were too young, then, she goes. You don't know. You don't remember. Do you know what I remember? Do you? I remember hearing you and Daisy being quiet. I remember hearing you playing, and then clambering up the stairs and telling each other to shush because Mammy was resting. I'd be lying there curled up as tightly as I could, so miserable I couldn't even move, couldn't even open my eyes, and I'd hear the sound of your wee feet padding across the floor and I'd feel you standing over me, and you'd whisper things like, It's going to be OK, Mammy, you'll feel better soon. It's going to be OK, Mammy! And I couldn't bear your being there. The part of me that was still awake wanted to scream at you to get the hell out and leave me alone. And sometimes, sometimes I wanted to shake you and shake you and tell you everything wasn't OK and it wasn't going to be OK. Your trusting wee faces.

She stops. Then, a moment later, she goes, There's fruit loaf for tea. They slice and butter it for you. Would we head back, then?

—What?

—They bake it fresh. Sometimes it's scones, drop scones, or a Victoria sponge, but it's fruit loaf today and you'll not do better than the barm brack you get here. Let's head back, then.

Oh, Jesus: there's so much I've wanted to talk about, so many things I've wanted to ask; and I've wanted to say sorry – I've needed to say sorry; I've wanted to say, Mammy, I'm sorry, I'm sorry for what happened, I should have been with Daisy, but please don't be cross at me any more, and even though it can't mend anything or change anything please let me say I'm sorry. There's so much, and I haven't said any of it.

—There's so much, I go. There's so much to say. To talk about.

—No, she hisses. No there's not. There's nothing to say. I always knew you'd come and find me one day, and I always dreaded that day because I knew what you'd say. The past is past, I tell you, and talking about it doesn't help. You have to lay it to rest. Turn your back on it and leave it behind.

—You can't leave your life behind, Mammy. It's like a shadow, I want to tell her. It trails behind you like a shadow and no matter how fast you jump or how suddenly you twirl around you can't trick it away.

—Saoirse, you've your life ahead of you. You can leave. I can't: I'm stuck here. Don't be feeling sorry for me, now. I'm not saying that to make you feel sorry for me. I'm – all right, here. It's peaceful. But I'm here, and you're not, and that's the way of it, and that's how it has to be.

—I don't understand, Mammy. I don't understand. You've been here for years. Years! Why? Why don't you just – leave? I don't understand.

—Enough! she spits, and her voice is hoarse. I'll not listen to another word. Not a single word, you hear me? It's not a hospital here, and it's not a prison, either. There're other women have been here far longer than me.

—But—

—What did I just say? One day I may well leave. One day. That's what I tell myself, sometimes. But then, then I have to ask myself, Where will I go? Where?

—Back to – to Gweebarra Sands.

She stares at me.

—Saoirse, you don't get it, do you? You don't get it. I can't bear – I can't be with you, Saoirse. I can't be around you, seeing you every day, because when I see you, I can't forget.

I grip the bench as hard as I can with both hands when she says that. It feels as if I am tumbling down, backwards and down. It feels as it felt when I fell from the fir tree, once, in Belfast, when I was climbing up to see some boys on the street hang bunting and I climbed too high and fell down, straight on to my back, and the fall knocked the air out of my lungs so badly that even when I managed to sit up I couldn't breathe. I think I am going to be sick, to boke up right in the middle of the nice neat lawn.

—Saoirse, my mother says. Saoirse.

I open my eyes and she's leaning towards me and her eyes are glassy; shining.

—Saoirse, she whispers. *Saoirse.*

Her face is inches from mine and I can feel the warmth of her breath. And then my mother moves away from me and clears her throat.

—Saoirse, before we go back, there's this I have for you. Carefully, she takes a plastic bag out of the pink and orange shopper. She sets it on my lap. The plastic bag is sellotaped up, and inside is a brown-papered parcel. And there's this, she says, holding out an envelope. I want you to have it, now. Open it.

It's a photograph: Daisy and I standing holding hands by the front door of our house in Belfast. The sun is bright behind us, coming in through the glass panel above the door, and we're slightly silhouetted. Our hair is neat, and our cheeks are pink and freshly scrubbed. Daisy's face is shiny and red, as if she's only after crying. But perhaps she was just excited. It must have been a special occasion. We're beaming up at the camera, standing proudly in what must be our best dresses, mine ridiculously flouncy with the lace of a petticoat showing underneath, and Daisy's bright pink with big yellow polka dots. Our skinny legs stick out like pipe-cleaners, and we're wearing white socks with frills and matching maroon T-bar sandals. All of a sudden, I remember having a tantrum in the shop when Mammy bought Daisy the exact same pair of shoes that I'd just chosen, and she had to drag me, gurning, the whole way back up the Sandy Row.

—Look at the two of youse, my mother says, and she strokes the photo with the tip of one finger.

—I don't have any photos, I whisper.

—We didn't bring them with us.

I stare at the shiny smiley faces.

—Don't be crying, now.

—I'm not crying, I go. I'm not crying.

Then I go, I'm sorry, Mammy, I'm so sorry.

I've said it.

Silence.

Then, You don't . . . you don't *blame* yourself, do you, she says, slowly, twisting her fingers in her lap.

—But it was my fault, Mammy! It was my fault you were cross with us in the first place. And then it was my fault I wasn't playing with Daisy. She wanted me to play with her and I wouldn't and she was all alone and I wasn't there to watch over her.

—You were only wee. The both of youse were only wee.

What have you done? How could you? Get away from me, go on, get away, I can't bear to touch you. Get away from me I said! What have you done, what have you done?

—You said . . . I falter.

—I said nothing! She turns on me, her face twisted. I can feel the flecks of spit landing on my cheeks. I said nothing! And you can't – you can't do this! I can't be – be held to account, yes, *held to account*, for anything I may have said in – in anger, or in grief, you hear me?

—But, Mammy, do you remember what you said?

—If I said anything, it was only words! Words! Only words! I'm saying now – I've just said, have I not? – I'm saying now, it wasn't your fault! Then she starts shaking. I can't do this, Saoirse, I can't. Don't make me, don't make me go back. I can't do it. I can't. I'm sorry. I'm sorry for everything. Sorry for all of it. I'm sorry.

—I'm sorry too, Mammy!

—Saoirse!

—No, you have to let me be sorry too! You have to let me be sorry, too!

We gulp our sorries out to each other; we keep on crying, Sorry, I'm sorry, over and over.

We are sitting side by side on the bench, almost touching, only a couple of inches between us.

I reach out, wanting to hug my mother, but her arms are wrapped tightly around herself, her hands clutching her shoulders.

When we've caught our breath back, and wiped our eyes and noses dry, we walk back up to the house, through the garden and the flower beds. Sister Mary Aloysius comes down to meet us on the steps of the Residents' Lounge.

—You've had a nice walk, then?

I nod, foolishly.

—We walked around the lake, I croak.

—You walked around the lake, did you? Well, and isn't that nice. She looks keenly at my face, and she looks at my mother's face, and she smiles a smooth smile. It's almost time for tea, Deirdre! she says in a voice as smooth as her smile. Will you help me sound the bell?

She's got a big brass hand-bell, like the kind Miss Deeny used to use in the playground. My mother takes it in both hands and shakes it, up and down, up and down, and the jerky chimes clang out across the garden.

I can see the Sister frowning at my red, puffy eyes and my swollen face, and when she sees that I've seen her displeasure she darts me a quick, tight, lopsided smile.

—I'm sorry if it's been difficult for you, she says, in a low voice. But I must say that I do hope you haven't upset your mother too much. Deirdre's mind is very delicate, you see. Perhaps it's best for both of you if you wait a while before coming again, yes? Give yourselves time to get used to things, you understand.

The ringing stops.

—Come then, Deirdre, and we'll say goodbye to Saoirse, will we, and then we'll go in for our tea, she says in her clear bright voice, taking my mother's arm as if my mother's a cripple.

I say, I thought—

—You can come for tea another time, perhaps, she says, quickly.

I look at my mother. My mother's face is blank and her eyes are the eyes of an idiot. And suddenly I'm angry. She's not a feckin' cripple! I want to shout. I want to shout, Stand up straight, Mammy! Get a grip!

Then I look again at her moony face where it's starting to sag at the jaw, with thready veins reddening the tip of her nose and lacing her cheeks and the whites of her eyes, and her eyes are pale and watery and she keeps blinking, too often and too quickly, and I think of when people used to say to me, You've yer mammy's eyes, and then I think what I haven't let myself think all afternoon: You're not my mammy any more. My mammy's long gone, gone way before that night of the broken shells and the screeching tyres on the drive, gone even before we arrived in Gweebarra Bay; away with the fairies, Daddy used to say, gently, when he came home and she was curled up in the brown sofa, sucking her little finger, the saucepans empty on the stove and dinner long forgotten, and me and Daisy dozing, curled up beside her, You're away with the fairies, arenten you? And a little voice inside of me says, But she was only young, then, she was only in her twenties and she missed her family, and No, I say, *no*, we were her family, *we* were, Daisy and I and Daddy, *we* were her family and she was my mammy but not any more.

—Shall we say goodbye, then? the Sister is saying.

There is a dull roaring in my head.

—Goodbye, I say, thickly.

—Bye, my mother says, blinking rapidly. Bye.

Later on, lying in my little box room with its painted moon and stars, I think of when we were little, and how Mammy was a magical storyteller. My room is stuffy. I reach up and push open the skylight, as far as it can go, and I lean out into the night. There is no wind, and no light, tonight, and the waters of Gweebarra Bay are cold and taut as the surface of a mirror.

I slide out of bed and cross the room, almost reluctantly, to where the plastic bag containing the brown paper parcel is sitting on my dresser. I pick it up. There is an envelope stuck to the outer layer of the parcel; *Saoirse*, it says, in carefully curly handwriting. I stare at it for a second, my name written in this unfamiliar handwriting, and then I set it to one side and start to open the parcel.

The sellotape is old and crackly, and peels away easily in brittle yellow flakes. There are several layers of paper, and I smooth them into a neat pile. I realize what is inside, of course, before the yellowy-cream leather is revealed; cracked, now. Slowly, I lift the music box from the final layer of paper and stroke the lid with one finger. I trace the embossed gold pattern that runs around the edges, and touch the tarnished gold catch. It is broken, and flops up with no resistance. I open the lid, and the white-and-gold ballerina springs up, ready to begin dancing, even after all these years. My fingers

194

find the knob at the back right-hand side, and move over it, but I hesitate, and do not turn it. I catch a glimpse of my face in the mirror, flushed red in the velvet lining, and I carefully close the lid.

20

My father comes down from Belfast, and for the first time, the first time ever, he and Aunt Bernadette sit round the same table, in the same room, under the same roof.

I hear his car arrive: the room is muggy and airless and my skylight is wide open, and so I hear his footsteps up the gravel drive and I hear my aunty open the back door and I hear her say, Welcome. And I know that I have to go down and face them. For the past couple of days, I haven't had the energy to get up. It's felt as if I'm floating, as if I'm sealed away somewhere; as if everything's happening still but none of it touches me and I'm just floating. It occurs to me: maybe this is a little bit how my mother felt. But I'm not my mother, and that thought, more than anything else, makes me able to get up.

My eyes are sore and prickly and my face is puffy. I feel groggy, and my arms and legs are heavy and slow. I lurch out of bed and stumble to the sink, and I wipe my face with a cold flannel, and comb my hair.

On my dressing table is a note from Johnny Mahon. A couple of evenings ago Mrs Mahon came round; vaguely, I heard raised voices in the kitchen as Aunt Bernadette told Úna Mahon exactly what she thought of her son, and her family. My aunty came up and said there was a note for me but if I had any sense I'd throw it straight away. I open it: *Sha*, it goes, in Johnny's scrawly writing, *I didn't want you to get in any trouble yeah at first I needed a reason to be seen over at*

Dennehy's but then we had some good craic didn't letting you down and your Ball and all, J.

I skim-read it, and toss it into the waste-paper basket, then I take a deep breath, and go downstairs.

—You've lost weight, my father says.

—She's not been eating, my aunty says to him.

—She looks like a ghost, my father says.

—What do you expect, Uncle Brendan says, suddenly, sharply, and neither of them says anything more, then. My uncle stands up, and pulls out a chair for me. Here you are, love.

He gives me a quick smile and squeezes my arm as I sit down beside him. It seems dead funny looking across the table at my father and my aunty, sitting side by side, awkward and polite. My aunty is holding her head high in a way that reminds me of my mother. It's strange, because Aunt Bernadette looks nothing like my mother. My aunty is a decade and a half older, for a start; she was born before the Second World War. I think, sometimes, she belongs to a different generation than my mother, a generation that must've made her old before her time. When my aunty was a teenager, things were just supposed to go on the way they always had. When my mother was a teenager, the sixties were in full swing and everything was – different.

My aunt glances at my father; their eyes meet. He coughs. She looks away.

—We know that you'll have a lot of questions, my father says, slowly, saying it like the beginning of a speech. We know that you'll be feeling—

—You know feck all about how I'm feeling, I interrupt.

—Language, my aunty goes, automatically.

—Fuck you, I say back at her.

Saoirse! says my father. You'll not speak to your aunt like that.

—Jesus, the two of youse've got pally. I hadn't realized I was so angry at them.

My father starts again.

—We'd like to explain to you—

—Let Saoirse talk, Uncle Brendan interrupts.

—I beg your pardon?

—I said, let Saoirse talk. I don't mean any offence now, but it seems to me that both you and my wife are still taking it upon yourselves to decide what to do, and what's right for her. All's I'm saying is, give Saoirse herself a chance to ask you questions, or to say what she wants to say.

Aunt Bernadette flares up at him: And who made you the mediator, Brendan?

—No, he's got a point, my father interjects. Saoirse—

But I cut across him, and it all comes out of me in a rush.

—You didn't see fit to tell me because you thought it would upset me, I go. So instead, you pretend for all these years that she just – disappeared, that she just upped sticks and left, and that you don't have the foggiest where she went, or what happened to her. How the hell can a lie like that be better than the truth?

—You would have wanted to see her, my aunty goes. You wouldn't have understood about the alcohol and the break-down and that. There was a long time when she didn't know who anyone was, or, at least, she didn't acknowledge anyone. And she— She breaks off.

—And she what?

—Nothing, pet. It was nothing.

—What were you going to say?

—She . . . she might not have wanted to see you.

198

I can't be around you, because when I see you, I can't forget.

I look from one face to another, from my father's to my aunty's and back to my father's again; they're looking at me with an expression I can't stand: sad, and pitying at the same time. And I'm furious at them thinking they know what's best for me; making decisions about me behind my back, and treating me like a child. I take a deep breath and sit up straight.

—I sort of understand your reasoning behind that, I say, quieter. But I think it was wrong of youse, letting me think – *making* me think – that my mother had run away on me. Had disappeared. The hours and hours I spent, wondering where she was, wondering if she'd ever come back, and all along, all along, you knew.

—We thought it was for the best! My aunty's voice is shrill. At the time, we thought it best to let you start a new life, to concentrate on your new school and your new – and your . . . She trails off.

—We couldn't've loved our own daughter more, is what your aunty wants you to understand, my uncle says.

I look at my father: his head is bowed.

—It seemed best, he goes, without looking up. Then he goes, You said to me, Saoirse, the other day you said to me why didn't I want you, all those years ago. And the answer is I did want you to stay in Belfast with me; I wanted desperately not to let you go, but it wasn't practical, it wasn't possible, the hours I was working, and suddenly with nowhere to live while we sold the house, and it made sense for you to stay with your mother—

—My alcoholic mother?

He doesn't say anything for a bit.

—When things spiralled out of control, Bernadette and I talked about whether you should come back to Belfast.

My aunt nods, slowly.

—But it seemed like you were just settling in here, and we didn't want more upheaval for you, and other officers in my line of work were being targeted; their houses were being petrol-bombed, their cars were being booby-trapped: and I'd come up here, and I'd see the beach for you to play on, and fields to run about in, and everything peaceful and far away from – trouble. From the Troubles. From politics.

—It's been trouble all my life, Da. Politics. If that's your word for it.

He goes to say something but I cut him off.

—And the other thing is, I don't understand how youse can let my mother be locked away there. How can you have let my mother be – be *locked away* for so many years? How?

—Your mother is ill, my father goes.

—She's terribly, terribly ill, my aunty adds. She's on very strong anti-depressive drugs, you know, and she still has bad days; days when she can't get herself up out of her bed, even. A couple of years ago she moved into a wee cottage in a village at the foot of the Blue Stacks. She had half of the cottage; there was an elderly couple lived in the other half. There were the views, and there were walks round Lough Eske, and it was only a short trip into the village. We thought it would be just the thing for her.

—When was this?

—Let's see now . . . three years ago, it'd be.

—When I was thirteen?

—Aye. Aye, you would've been about that age.

—Yeah, 'cause you were dead jippy with me for no reason back then.

—You were a teenager, Saoirse! It was you was in a foul mood most of the time. Hormones!

—Don't you hormones me. And anyway, what happened? Why did she not stay there?

—She couldn't do it. At first, it was fine. And there was talk of . . . well, talk of taking you to visit her. Although I didn't know if that would be a good thing. But then she started on the drink again.

—Hang on a second, I go. So how often did you go and see her, ey? And you, Da. Did you make secret wee trips up to visit her as well?

—Ach, love, he goes. I haven't seen your mother in years. I'm not – I'm not proud of that now. I went to La Retraite, at the beginning, a couple of times, but she refused to see me, and the – the nuns suggested it distressed her too much.

—Jesus, it's like, it's like we're in *Victorian* times or something. Secluding her! Secreting her away! Pretending that if something's hidden well enough it doesn't exist.

—Saoirse, pet, she's got people all around her, people to talk to, you know. Sure, what would she be doing here, for example? All day, ey? Stuck out here miles from nowhere with only myself and Brendan for company, for it's soon you'll be going, heading off to one of the cities, won't you, to study. She couldn't live here. You know yourself that outside of the holiday season there's barely enough work for one person.

I think of my uncle helping Manus out in low season, doing odds and ends about the farm, supplementing his pension in the months when there's no guests and no trout-fishing trips. I think of how shabby Gweebarra Sands is looking, these days, and how the farm's crumbling down around us.

Everyone has fallen silent, as if there's nothing more to say.

There's one more thing. Still somewhere in the back of my mind is this image of my father as a big brave strong man, coming in from the cold in his thick herringbone overcoat, and Daisy and I scampering downstairs and leaping up at him and burying our faces in that cold, rough coat that smelled of frost and darkness. And somewhere, despite everything that's happened, somewhere he still exists; despite the fact that this man who comes up to take me out for dinner, he's not big or strong or brave any more, and we can't even think of enough things to say to each other to fill an evening; despite all that, somewhere there still exists my father who'd tell us not to worry because so long as he was there nothing and nobody could harm us. He was wrong, of course. But even so, the memory of him is still there, somewhere.

—Daddy, I go. Daddy. You loved Mammy. Why was that not enough to – to keep us together? Why did you not – why *could* you not – try harder?

—I knew she was drinking, but . . . He spreads his hands wide, pleadingly, and then clenches his fingers into fists before sagging backwards into his chair. There was no talking to her. I just didn't know what to do. Every time we tried to talk it would escalate into an argument. I hoped it would pass, I hoped that with the end of the marching season, when things got back to normal, everything would right itself. And then, then things just spiralled out of control. Her best friend, I forget what you call her, her best friend left the country in horrible circumstances, and your mammy took it really badly. You probably don't remember much about that summer, that heatwave summer when everything fell apart, but it was a terrible time. Francis, his name was. Your mammy's friend's husband. He was shot by some Loyalist paramilitary splinter group, and your mammy . . .

He sighs, heavily.

—Deep down, I think she blamed me for it. I mean, it was

nothing to do with me, not in any reasonable way, and she'd never say anything outright, but I always felt she somehow held me responsible. And . . . well, and who else are you going to blame, ey? You blame the politics, but that isn't enough, and you blame the gunmen, but you don't know them. And as soon as you can put faces to them, they become ordinary people. Deirdre was terribly unhappy in Belfast, love, but – where else? Where else was there, ey, where could we possibly have gone? Neither of us really wanted to leave Ireland, but where in the Republic was an RUC man going to get employment? And, besides, we couldn't afford to move. There was you and – and Daisy, we were a wee – a wee— His voice is choked. He coughs several times, and continues in a rush. Our house would have brought us nothing at all; not the area it was in. It was completely impossible, the idea of moving away from Belfast.

None of us speaks for ages. You can hear the cooing of the pigeons that are scuffling and bumping about on the kitchen roof, in the warmth at the top of where the Aga pipe comes out.

—I tried to talk to her, but what could you do? my father suddenly continues. I was out a lot of the time; I'd come back and she wouldn't let me touch her—

—Colin, my aunty goes.

My father stops, abruptly.

—Sorry, he goes. Sorry. I – I forgot myself there for a second. Remembering.

My uncle lifts the pot to pour more tea, but nobody's touched their cup. He sets the pot down again, carefully, and I watch him straightening out the tea-cosy; it's the old red and yellow one I knitted in my final year of primary school, and he picks at the wool where it's unravelling.

—It was Isabella, I go.

—You what?

—Isabella. Mammy's friend. That was her name. Do you know what happened to her?

—Haven't a clue, love. She was your mother's friend. From a Mothers and Toddlers group, or something like that, I think. I was always trying to get Deirdre to get out and meet people. It wasn't easy on me, either, he goes, suddenly. It wasn't easy on anyone.

My father's not staying the night. My aunty has made colcannon, but none of us is hungry, and my father spoons it about a bit before saying that he should get going, as he has to get back to Belfast, and Pauline.

—Hey, I go, as it suddenly occurs to me.

What I want to ask is, had he met Pauline *then* – the nights he did not come home – and was he . . . But I look at my father and I suddenly think: I don't want to know. There's too much; if you let it, the story would go on for ever, and at some point it has to stop.

So I just go: Nothing. It doesn't matter.

I'm lying on my bed, just staring at the ceiling, when Aunt Bernadette taps on the door. I don't say anything, but she comes in anyway, and I can't be bothered to pretend I'm sleeping.

—I want to tell you the rest, she goes.

I shrug one shoulder, and turn away.

—It's too late, now. I don't care any more.

—But you should know, Saoirse.

I don't care; I don't know why, I just don't care any more.

—Please let me tell you.

—All right, I go. If you like.

She sits down on the edge of the bed.

—It was my fault, in a way, she goes, abruptly. I told our parents, Saoirse, and Deirdre never forgave me for that. But I thought I was doing the right thing, you see. I found out from our cousins in Letterkenny that Deirdre hadn't been staying with them at all, and I confronted her, said if she didn't tell me what was going on I'd tell our mother and father, and she confessed about going up to Derry, about the marches and all, and then, finally, about seeing your father. I think it was a relief for her, you know, because for near two years she'd been having this double life, almost. We weren't ever particularly close, me and Deirdre, especially not after I got married; she was scornful, I think; she didn't understand how I could be content to stay in Gweebarra Bay, because she had all these great plans, you see: one day it would be Dublin she'd be heading for, the next London, the next New York. Ah, the great ideas she had; and, you know, I really believed she'd do it. I was always a wee bit envious of her, deep down; not that I admitted it, of course, because she was our father's favourite – he'd let her get away with murder, so he would – and she was . . . she was the type of person could walk into a room and that room would suddenly be brighter. That sounds like a terrible auld cliché, but it's true, that's what Deirdre was like. Anyways, she said she'd break it off with your father, but she didn't, and at Christmastime, the Christmas before she left, Brendan and I had come here to spend the holiday, and we were sleeping in Deirdre's room, and – well, to cut the story short, I happened to find letters your father had written her. They were inside of a jewellery box that she'd left unlocked. And I think part of me was hurt she hadn't told me. And – Jesus, Saoirse, I'm not proud of it – I showed the letters to our mother. I just thought Deirdre was throwing her life away, getting involved with a Prod from the forces; and actually, it wasn't the religious thing so much as, well, at the end of nineteen-seventy, things just looked like they were getting worse and worse; there was talk that we were heading for outright civil war, and I thought Deirdre was getting herself in too deep. She was only nineteen; she was still a teenager. My mother pleaded with Deirdre, and in the end Deirdre promised on the family Bible not to see Colin again. I wasn't there when she left. Mother told me, afterwards, what happened, but by then it was too late. There was a showdown, around Eastertime; I don't know what triggered it, but my father found out what was going on, and he found out that we'd known and been concealing it from him. He had an awful temper on him, our father; he wasn't a cruel man, but you didn't want to get on the wrong side of him. And he slapped Deirdre across the face and he said a lot of unforgivable things. And my mother was crying, and Deirdre rushed upstairs, and when she came down she was carrying her little brown overnight bag, and she stood in the doorway, and our father said – ach it was terrible, I remember it as clear as yesterday – he said, without looking up from his paper, 'Deirdre Mary O'Conor, if you walk out that door, you'll no longer be a daughter of mine.'

—And Deirdre looked across at our mother, and our mother wouldn't meet her eye. And so Deirdre just left, and none of us said anything. Eventually my father threw down the paper and said that she'd come to her senses and be back soon enough, and he stormed off to the pub. He was heartbroken, so he was. He never talked about her, when it became clear she wasn't coming back; he never mentioned her name, but he wasn't the same after she left. There, she finishes, with a deep breath, I've told you now.

I close my eyes.

—Saoirse? she goes.

—I want to be on my own now, I go. But she doesn't leave.

—Saoirse, she goes. Saoirse, when you came here, you were like a wee ghost. You never spoke or anything. You just watched everyone with big scared eyes. It near enough broke my heart, seeing you creep around the place like the slightest puff of wind would blow you away. All's I've wanted – all's your uncle and I have wanted – is for you to be happy here.

She falls silent.

—I'm sorry, love, she says. I'm so sorry.

21

It's been waiting there for almost a week, now, the letter, in its cheap white envelope with its curlicued *Saoirse* in that careful and slightly cramped handwriting. Once or twice a day I've picked it up: it is thick; the letter inside must cover several sheets of paper. If I hold it up to the light I can make out the faint shape of words through the thin envelope, but I cannot read any of them. It's not that I've been scared of the letter, not exactly; it's more that once I've read it, then I'll know what it has to say.

I go down to the beach to read it, where I won't be disturbed, where I'll be alone. The wind is making patterns, swirling over the wild grasses and flattening the long strands this way and then that, sending little puffs of sand scudding. I climb down into the lee of the sand dunes on the right-hand side of the shore, and on to the rocks beyond, where it's more sheltered, and where I'm hidden from sight. And I open my mother's letter.

Dear Saoirse,

I am writing you this letter because I know that one day you will come and find me, and you will come with questions which I am unable to answer, questions to which, perhaps, there are no answers; and so in explanation, or rather, in an attempt at explanation, I am writing this letter for you.

I reread the first sentence a couple of times, and I hear it in my mother's voice: smooth, distant, carefully controlled. Her storytelling voice, I think, suddenly; she's writing to me in her storytelling voice: *in at attempt at explanation, I am writing this letter for you*; and I wish, I wish with all my heart that I'd known my mother, because whatever her letter says, it's words, it's only words, and it's too late, now.

You must understand, Saoirse: you must understand that I did not intend to abandon you; I never intended to <u>desert</u> you; I was ill, and I hardly knew who I was or what was going on around me, and so I cannot be held fully responsible for my behaviour at the time. My life had turned to dust around me; my daughter was dead, my marriage had failed, I had lost everything that I had fought for. I wanted to go to university, you know; I wanted to do things, to live: everyone always said that I'd go far. And I threw it all away to run up North and marry your father. I thought I was escaping; the day I left Gweebarra Bay, I thought I was finally free. And instead I ended up begging my older sister and her husband to take me in, and sleeping in a back room in the old family home I'd run away from. I wanted to be <u>new</u>; I wanted to start over again; I wanted to have my life over again; and instead I had about me the tattered remnants of a life already lived.

What about me, Mammy, I say, inside my head. Was I not enough? You had me: were the two of us not enough?

I loathed, Saoirse, I <u>loathed</u> myself. I hope to God you never know what that feels like. Imagine the moments when you're waking up, but you're not quite awake; those floating moments before you <u>remember</u> anything. Now, in those moments, in those moments before I even knew who or where I was, all that I did *know was that I hated myself, that I disgusted myself. It wasn't just the drink. It was something deeper than the drink.*

I came to see you, once. It was about a year after I left. I was dry; I'd finished the intensive rehabilitation programme, and I had come to La Retraite to convalesce; I didn't intend to stay there, then. I got the bus out, and it set me down in the centre of town at around lunchtime, and I walked up to Holy Trinity; I was hoping to meet you, I think, when you came out of school. I sat on a low wall just across from the playground, and I watched all of the children spilling out when the bell rang, and I looked for you, and I couldn't see you; I remember that I couldn't see you, at first. And then there you were: running straight towards me, your hair flying out behind you, one arm outstretched, the palm of your hand turned upwards.

I don't remember; I don't remember. For the flicker of a second I see me from outside of me – me *then*, scampering about the playground – but it's a false memory; it's my mother's memory, not mine, and to think that she was there watching me gives me a cold, lurching feeling in my stomach.

You didn't see me; you reached the railings of the playground, and turned and ran back in the other direction, still with one arm outstretched. I remembered how, in primary school, we were taught that our own personal guardian angel was always at our side, and we used to walk around holding its hand, everywhere we went, holding the imaginary hand of our invisible angel; I remembered that, and I wondered if Miss Deeny had taught you, too, to hold your angel's hand. It was then that I knew I couldn't do it; I couldn't go back. I said goodbye to you, then, in my heart; I said goodbye and then I sat and watched until Miss Deeny came out of the building and rang the bell and everyone lined up ready

to go back into school. That was just before I had my second
breakdown, and that time, I was much worse, for much longer;
and when I began to come out of it, I knew that you were better
off with Bernadette and Brendan, whom it was painfully clear
loved you like their own daughter, for what sort of a mother
could I ever be? I didn't intend to leave you, but I did: and you
must not think of me any more, Saoirse. You have your own life
to be living. Your name means freedom. *I chose it carefully.*

She signs the letter, *Deirdre.* That's all: not *Mammy*, not *your
mother*, even; just – *Deirdre*.

Later on, back in the kitchen of Gweebarra Sands, I rip the
letter into tiny pieces and stuff the pieces into the smoul-
dering range and clang the metal door shut. But even as the
words turn to dust and ashes I can still hear my mother's
voice echoing round and around in my head.

Go away! I want to scream. Please! Please let me be.

*I came to see you, once. I didn't intend to leave you, but I did.
You must not think of me any more.*

It isn't about you! I yell then, at the top of my voice, as if
by shouting loud enough she can somehow hear me. You tell
me to forget, but how can I forget?

This is my story, Mammy, my story: so why does it feel as
if I'm telling yours?

A parcel arrives in the post from Belfast. *Some bits and pieces,*
my father writes. *You can work out their stories for yourself.*

Inside the parcel is an old green Clarks shoebox, lined with
pages from the *East Belfast Newsletter.* The First World War
medal that my father told me about – another lifetime ago,
it seems – is in a shabby black box with a spring-catch. Inside,

the box is lined with padded white satin that's stained faintly yellow with age. The medal is heavy; brass-coloured; slightly tarnished. On the front is a picture of an angel, its right arm outstretched, pointing into the distance, and on the back it says, 'THE GREAT WAR FOR CIVILISATION 1914–1919'. On the rim, like you get on a pound coin, is engraved, 'William Stanley Pentland'.

Next, folded up in tissue paper, is an Orange Order collaret. It is a length of bright-blue-coloured, heavy silken cloth about four inches wide, with gold fringing, like a scarf. I hold it up to my neck; there is a shiny medallion to join the two ends together, inscribed with some lettering that I can't decipher, and a Lodge number. I remember hearing the music of the marching bands at the bottom of our road, how the beat of the drums and the quick catchy tunes of the pipes made you want to stamp along in time; how Daisy and I played at marching around the rug For God and Ulster in the hallway until Mammy caught us and told us off. For crying out loud, she shouted, it's bad enough they're marching in our street without the two of youse doing it in here.

There are a handful of telegrams, still in their little envelopes: the first one is dated March and it says, *Colin stop urgent stop will telephone tonight stop Deirdre*. The second is dated early April, and it says, *C stop have decided yes stop your D*; and the third, a couple of days later, says, *Arriving York Street station seven pm stop our life together begins exclamation mark exclamation mark stop love always stop*.

There is a Polaroid photo of them, of Mammy and Daddy, standing outside the City Hall in Belfast. *The Bride & Groom, Easter 1971*, it says on the bottom, in biro. My mother is wearing a Laura Ashley-print milkmaid dress that reaches almost to the ground. It's red and orange, with a pattern of green leaves and tiny blue flowers over it, and it has a high neckline with a standy-up ruffled collar. Her hair is long and loose, slightly wavy, and she's laughing, clutching my father around the waist. Looking at the photo, there's nothing to tell that she's five months pregnant with me. She looks dead young; she was barely twenty, then, and she looks younger than that, even. My father is wearing a brown suit with flared trousers, and a wide yellow tie. His hair is curly and reaches down to his shoulders, and he's got a thick moustache. He doesn't look like my father at all. He's smiling down at my mother, and he's got one arm around her shoulders. If you ignore the seventies clothes she's wearing, it could be me in that photo, I think, and it's a funny feeling.

Then, finally, there is a card which says *Happy Father's Day* and inside my mother has printed, in childlike writing, *See you in just over a month. I know you're going to be a Great Dad and we're going to be so happy, love from Me xoxoxo.*

That's me, I think.

There's nothing of Daisy's in there. I pack them carefully back in the shoebox, these little pieces of a past that's mine and not mine.

22

A couple of days later, in Melly's for the first time in ages, I say to Bridget and Mairead and a few of the others, My great-grandfather was killed on the Somme. Him and three of his brothers on the one day.

—Really? Bridget goes. Jaysus.

—Aye, I go. They were Orangemen.

The others look at me. Yeah, I think, it makes me different. All of my life here I've wanted so badly to be the same. But now, I'm kind of proud to be an Ulster Pentland as well as an O'Conor from the Gaeltacht.

—Hey, Mairead goes. Did youse hear, Johnny Mahon might get off without a jail sentence. On account of how he's young and he's an accessory or something.

I shrug.

—Arenten you glad?

—Glad?

—Well, arenten you?

I suppose so. I suppose I'm glad he'll get another chance. But it's nothing to do with me. I'll be having nothing to do with him again. He had his choice, and he made it. I say that, and the others are silent.

Then I say, I'm going to go up North for a week. Before school starts.

—Up *North*? Bridget goes.

—To Belfast.

—*Belfast?* one of the others goes.

—Are you off your bap?

—But the bombs and all, are you not scared?

—I can't be scared, I go. I'm half from there. I can't be scared.

I pass my driving test a fortnight after I turn seventeen. Since Easter, Manus Dennehy has been letting me practise manoeuvres in one of the fallow fields joining on to our garden. My uncle painted out car parking spaces and right angles and taught me three-point turns and reversing round corners and what have you, so I can already drive pretty well by the time I'm legally allowed on the roads.

—Congratulations, says the examiner. You're free to go wherever you want, now.

My aunty makes me sandwiches, and packs them neatly in a Tupperware box with a tinfoiled wedge of buttered barm brack, and she gives me an envelope with two hundred pounds sterling in. I know fine well we can ill afford it. But she insists.

—For the petrol and what have you, she goes.

—Thank you, Aunty, I go.

—My pleasure, Niece, she says, in a funny sort of way.

—Aunty, I go.

One afternoon, when I'd been a few months at Gweebarra Sands, Aunt Bernadette took me on her knee.

—If you like, you can call me Mam, she said. She added, quickly, Only Aunt Bernadette's a bit of a mouthful.

—Thank you, Aunt Bernadette, I said, and I wriggled out of her arms and ran upstairs. She never brought it up again.

—Yes love, she says, softly, and she smooths my hair.

—Nothing, I go, kind of flustered. Then I try again: Aunty,

it's not that – I mean it's not that you and Uncle Brendan weren't, you know . . .

—It's all right, love, she says, quietly. I understand. I understand. Then she kisses me on the forehead. You'd best be on your way, she goes. Take care, love. Good luck.

Then, just as I am leaving, she calls me back.

—You can't forget what's happened, she says, carefully, but you can't spend your life remembering, *instead*.

I meet her gaze for a split second, then turn away.

PART THREE

Greyabbey

23

The North is a different country. Even the roads feel different: narrowed, smoother, with different markings. I drive up through Letterkenny and cross the border just outside Derry, where the cars slow to a crawl, queuing to get through the British Army checkpoint. Every now and then a car is made to pull over to the verge, and the boot and bonnet are inspected. If you go into a shop in the North, Aunt Bernadette said, the soldiers'll rummage through your handbag before they let you over the threshold. Wee girls, even, and even old women: nobody gets off.

I have my driving licence ready, and in my head I rehearse saying, Aye, I'm going up to Belfast to visit relatives, because I'm worried that it'll sound stilted; false. I'm going up North to visit relatives. I prepare myself for questions; but when it comes to my turn, the soldiers wave me through uninterestedly.

Uncle Brendan told me to cross the Governor's Bridge and take the ring road around the city: don't drive through, was the last thing he said. Make sure you don't drive through for you'll get snarled up in traffic and you might well get lost in the one-way system. And you don't want to be lost in the Waterside (or was it the Bogside, did he say?) with Southern number plates. Lock your doors, he said. Keep your doors locked and keep your eyes peeled and don't be taking any chances. Just bypass Derry and get yourself straight on to the motorway.

But I want to see the city where my mother marched, where my mother and father met; and so I follow the signs for the Historic Walled City Centre and I take the bridge across the Foyle.

You can drive right underneath the old stone arches where the gates were, where the thirteen Apprentice Boys shut Ferrygate just minutes before King James and his Catholic forces would've stormed the city. The traffic is snarled up almost to a standstill, and there's nowhere to park; I inch round the old centre a couple of times, craning out of the window and snatching glimpses of the Cathedral spire above me, at the highest point on the hill; and, looming behind it, the Army Observatory Tower, a tangle of barbed wire and metal grilles and CCTV cameras. Rain clouds are low in the sky, and everything is grey and dull; even the people have grey, dull expressions on them; but there are occasional splashes of red and blue and yellow on the road: the marks of paint bombs, they must be, I realize with a shock, but what it looks like is as if giant-sized little children have gone mad finger-painting.

I take the right turn out of the one-way system, and on the road back down the hill, I can see the Republican enclave, clusters of terraced houses hunched to the ground in the wasteland between the walled city and the Donegal country-side, many of them painted in pretty pastel colours, with oversized Tricolour flags fluttering above the bold murals of dancing girls and balaclava'd men brandishing guns that are painted on the end of every row of houses and on every wall. Imagine having to live with an ugly big mural on your house, I think, and I remember suddenly how Daisy and I begged Mammy to let us help paint Cúchulainn, Ancient Defender of Ulster against Irish Attacks, at the bottom of our street.

Paused at the traffic lights on the edge of the city, I read the infamous sign in my rear-view mirror, the sign that's used time and time again as a backdrop in news bulletins: 'You are Now entering Free Derry'. When my mother was my age, she was just about to meet my father, and the Troubles hadn't even begun. And then the car behind me beeps, and the lights have changed to green, and I'm driving on, on to the Glenshane Pass, which will take me over the Sperrin Mountains, and it's easy from then on in, said Uncle Brendan, because you don't have to leave the road; the same road that takes you past Magherafelt and over the River Bann becomes a motorway a few miles outside of Toome, and goes all the way past Antrim and Newtownabbey and then into Belfast. You can't go wrong, he said. You can't get lost. It's an easy journey.

From Toome to Belfast is only thirty miles. The word on the signs gets bigger and more frequent: 'Belfast, The South'; 'West Belfast'; 'East Belfast'; 'Belfast'; 'BELFAST'; 'WELCOME TO BELFAST'.

I think of how, when Daisy and I were wee, 'Belfast' was the game that the older girls on our street played in the long summer evenings as we watched from our hidey-hole between the biggest fir tree and the hedge. Ring the bell and run away fast as yer legs'll carry you: that's Bell-fast for you. The girls'd take turns choosing houses for each other to do, making chicken noises and shouting, Cowardy cowardy custert, yer daddy's made of mustert, if someone refused to take their turn. They never did our house because the metal gate was heavy and squeaked too much. But sometimes they did our neighbour's, an old lady, she was, who'd make me and Daisy giggle by juking over the hedge like a shrivelledy auld jack-in-the-box when she heard our father in the garden, and calling our father wee love and wee son. Be kind to her, Sunshine, my father told me one day when I couldn't for the life of me stop giggling. She's lost her husband and son, and she gets lonely.

The girls playing Belfast would be long gone by the time our old neighbour – Mrs Mildred, we called her, Mouldy Mildred – opened the door, and she'd shuffle to the bottom of her wee drive and curse at the empty street. *Yer fly bints the lot of yez would yez ever stop minchin' into my garden have yer mammies and daddies not learned youse any respect?*

Safely hidden away, Daisy and I used to laugh at the way that auld woman'd be shaking her walking stick at the air and shouting in her quavery voice, craning her neck out to see if she could spot any of the bould girls that'd been ringing her doorbell; but deep down, I think we were always a little bit scared of the time when we'd be old enough to play Belfast.

I'm on the outskirts of the city when it hits me, hard: the realization that I don't quite know how to think of Daisy any more, because when I think of me and Daisy it is always *then*, of course, when I am not-quite-seven and she is only-just-four. It seems so obvious, so silly; and yet it hasn't quite occurred to me like that before.

I almost miss the turning but I manage to change lanes just in time, and then I'm on to the Sydenham Bypass and following the signs for Newtownards. You're almost there, I say out loud to myself.

It's late afternoon by the time I'm on the southern outskirts of Newtownards, and heading down the Ards Peninsula, a thin finger of land that curves down around Strangford Lough and reaches out into the Irish Sea. The road runs right beside the Lough, and I pull over on to a bit of gravel by the verge to stop for a rest and eat Aunt Bernadette's sandwiches. I'm knackered: I can't stop thinking about things and remembering silly little things like playing Belfast that I thought I'd forgotten.

I get out of the car and clamber over a couple of boulders to get to the water's edge. It's brightened up, and under the late afternoon sun the rocks and waters are shining, and the little rippling waves are silvery and translucent, swelling in and out against the thin band of rocky shore. It's pretty, really pretty. When you think of the North you don't think of it as being pretty; you tend to think only of bombs and things like barbed wire and concrete barriers in the rain, but here by the edge of the Lough is one of the prettiest places I've seen.

Back in the car, I look at my uncle's map of County Down and the Ards Peninsula. Last night he showed me on a map how to get to East Belfast.

—Would you have another map? I asked. A more detailed one?

—You'll not need a more detailed one. Stormont's easy enough to find, and your father's written directions from there, has he not?

—Yes, but I just want to know how to get to . . . Well. Greyabbey and that. Those parts.

—I'm sure your father'll take you if you ask him. You don't want to be getting yourself lost, now. You'd be best off just concentrating on getting to your father's.

—Uncle Brendan, I don't want my father to take me there. I want to – I have to – go there by myself, first.

He looked at me for a moment, tilting his head to one side, and I felt myself flush. But he fetched the map without another word.

On the back of the map is a short guide to the area, and

it says that when St Patrick came to Ireland this is where his wee leather curragh is supposed to have landed. We learned in primary school how he laid down the oars when he saw the land of his former captivity, and as he struggled to put aside his grief, it was the will of God carried the little boat to the shore. This narrow stretch of land, the guide goes, is layered with the ruins of its tumultuous past, remnants of the waves of battling Christians and Norsemen which periodically swept across it, each age bringing anew the building and the burning of abbeys and churches, towers and kilns. Nowadays, the call of the tern has replaced the screams of battle, it says, and mass burial pits are no more than slight dips in green fields: history is at rest, finally, grassed over by the quiet centuries.

It's time to be getting on. I follow the map to a little town near the ruins of Greyabbey Monastery, where I stop and ask in a newsagent's for proper directions: many of the roads round these parts are not signposted, and they twist round and join back on to themselves, so you can all too easily end up at an earlier place than where you started. There are a few strings of bunting still hanging between the lampposts, left over from the July parades, and in the upstairs windows of several houses I see purple-and-orange UDA flags, the Red Hand of Ulster slapped defiantly across them. I am suddenly very conscious of the Southern touch to my accent, and of the Donegal registration plates on the car; two women in the newsagent's narrow their eyes and look at me with guarded curiosity when I begin to speak, and I am glad to hurry on. I am a Greyabbey Pentland, I want to say; I belong here, too; but like Derry, this isn't a familiar place, either. And so I decide not to stop and see the old abbey. Time's getting on, and I don't want to be disappointed: one of our favourite stories that our father used to tell us was set in Greyabbey, about him and his friends, when *they* were the age of me and Daisy, playing up in the ruins of the old Cistercian monastery. They played hide and seek, he said, and soldiers, and sometimes they had themselves a game of football on the grass behind the skeleton of the chapel. But when twilight began to fall, they'd stop whatever they were doing and run home: because at night, in the moonlight, the pale walls and high arches of the Abbey gleamed like smooth yellow bones. Once, he'd say, lowering his voice to a hoarse whisper, the cousin of a friend of his saw a shadow moving towards him, and as it got closer he saw that it was no shadow, but the figure of a monk in a dark brown cowl, and it was gliding across the lawn, coming straight for him.

—He couldn't move, he couldn't scream, he couldn't even *breathe*, my father would say, bending closer towards me and Daisy huddling together in my bed.

It wasn't only my mother who was a good storyteller: listening to my father, I knew exactly how that boy must have felt, because I couldn't breathe, either.

—Then, my father would continue, then the friend's cousin noticed something that made his *blood run cold*. The ghostly friar was buried to his knees, and yet he was still sliding, not over, but *through* the lawn!

That was the point at which Daisy and I would start screaming and squealing with pleasure and fear.

—No more, Daddy, no more! Daisy would shout.

—Did he get away, Daddy? Tell us how he got away! I would shout over her.

—He said his prayers! said our father. His voice came back to him and he closed his eyes and gabbled his prayers as loud as he could, and when he'd finished, the ghost was gone!

225

It's a quare thing, I think, suddenly, how my father, who rubbished all talk of church and religion, calling it Magicking Nonsense, would end our favourite story with the wee boy saved by saying his prayers. Then I think how my father was raised a good Presbyterian lad, and I think how maybe you can never really get away from where you come from.

24

The little church is on the most southerly point of the peninsula, down a narrow lane that's overgrown with cow parsley and long wild grass, and bordered on each side by gently sloping fields. I park in a lay-by to the side of the road, and I sit there for a bit. I can see gravestones through the trees, and I can see the church huddled to the ground, its plain spire hardly any higher than the trees surrounding it.

All of a sudden I remember with absolute clarity standing right there outside the church, and the minister coming over to my mother and taking her hand and saying, It's with great dignity you're bearing yourself in this time of loss.

I remember precisely how he said it, and I remember how my mother stared at him with utter incomprehension.

Then I remember back to the service itself; how the altar was heaped with lilies, and how the scent hung heavy in the air and a lady behind me kept sneezing. How streams of dust fell in the light from the high windows, and how, outside, the shapes of two pigeons bumped against the back of the blue and amber saint. I remember wriggling and swinging my legs because the stiff T-bars of my new sandals were buckled too tight, and I remember how my tights itched where the backs of my legs were sweaty against the varnish of the pew, and how a few hairs in my half-ponytail pulled at the nape of my neck. I remember looking around at the people there, people I didn't know; and I watched my father staring into space, not noticing when everyone else got to their feet, and I watched my mother, her eyes small and puffy and bruised. I remember all of this, as if it's only just happened, as if it's only just happening. The final prayer was Patrick's prayer that Mammy taught us to say at night after we went to church that time: *Christ be with me, Christ within me, Christ behind me, Christ beside me, Christ to win me.* I can almost hear, now, the minister intoning it, and I think how when he got to *Christ in hearts of all that love me*, my mother's fingers gripped my wrist so hard I whimpered, and how, as he came to the end of the prayer, and the end of the service, she sank back in the pew, suddenly limp, and she swayed back and forth, a low, awful noise coming from her slack mouth, and I began to feel scared.

There's not another soul about. I stay sitting in the car for I don't know how long, and I think of my father and my mother and how much has happened and I wonder: at what point was there no turning back? And I feel suddenly dizzy with the thoughts of it all.

I don't seem to be able to get out of the car. You have to go now, I tell myself, you've come this far, but I can't seem to leave, somehow. My whole body is heavy with tiredness. Just a little longer, then, I tell myself; you can stay here a little bit longer, but soon you're going to have to go.

I find Daisy's grave in a sheltered corner, where two crumbling stone walls meet, and the lowest branches of an old stooped oak tree droop over the walls and lean, swaying slightly, towards the earth. The gravestone has a carved angel on top of it, and it says: *In Hope.*

I pick the dirt out of where it's caked into the carved letters, and I trace the name with my fingers; I remember when I saw it, and how I screamed and cried because they'd written

Aideen Pentland: Daisy had never been Aideen, even to my mother, who insisted that her girls had Irish names. Daisy: she'd always, always been Daisy. I spelled it out, and the name was my proof: I knew that they'd made a mistake, that Daisy wasn't meant to go in there. When I started up guldering, my mother smacked me round the back of the legs and shouted, For shame! Shame on you! which made me shriek even more, and my father carried me thrashing and struggling to the car, where he strapped me in without a word and then sat there staring straight ahead.

—Hiya, Daisy, I go. It's me, Sunshine.

Then I say, Remember the red lights at the top of Samson and Goliath and how we used to think they were the torches at the entrance to the Castle in the Sky?

Then I say, I brought you something.

I feel a wee bit stupid doing it; I can imagine how if my aunty could see me she'd be shaking her head and going, Are you off of your bap?

But I do it anyway: I set the music box carefully on the earth and even though the catch is broken, now, I open the lid. Then, suddenly, I start to giggle at myself: what are you like, girl, I think, imagining the face of the minister or the caretaker or whoever, coming down into the graveyard and seeing, instead of a bunch of flowers or what have you, an auld busted music box lying there.

I lean back against the wall. The dusk air is cool and damp. I sit there until the gravestones are soft dark shadows, and then I get up and say, I'm going to make tracks now.

25

It is late, and my father and Pauline will be wondering where I am. I stop at a garage payphone, and ring their number. My father picks up almost immediately, and I can hear Pauline in the background going, Is it her, is everything OK?

—Hiya Daddy, I say. It's me, it's taken a while, but I'm almost there.

—Well, you're better late than never, he goes. We were beginning to think you'd decided against it after all. Turned back.

—No.

There is a short pause.

—Good, he says, softly. I'm glad. And then, slightly awkwardly, We're – we're all looking forward to seeing you.

—OK, I say. See you soon; and as I go to hang up the phone there is a muffled noise in the background: the sound of a baby crying. Da, I go, Da, is that—

—Aye, he goes, and I can hear the smile in his voice. That's wee Amy-Rose, she's been keeping us up all night the past few nights, so she has.

Oh my goodness, I think, for the first time, that's my wee sister: I've got a baby sister.

—Saoirse, love, are you still there?

I start to say: Yes, I'm still here; but the payphone cuts out before I've said it and I stand, dazed, for a few seconds, blinking in the fluorescent yellow lights of the garage forecourt.

It's not fair, is the thought drumming round and round inside my head. That wee baby is going to have everything. And all I want, then, and for a split second I want it more than I've ever wanted anything in my whole life, all I want is to start again, for everything to start again, new and clean—

If I left now, I think – suddenly – I could be home by the morning. I could be—

I turn away abruptly, and hurry towards the car, my heart beating fast. There is a dull, choking, familiar tightness in my chest.

My hand is on the car door and I am fumbling with the keys when something makes me pause, and turn around, and look back in the direction of the Lough. In the brief time it took to make the phone call to my father, night-time has settled over Belfast, and the last lingering streaks of light are fading fast from the sky. Clouds are rolling in from the north, from the channel; already the air tastes damp; it will rain tomorrow, I think.

I shiver, and climb into the car.

I drive back over the Craigantlet hills, and as I come to the final rise, all of Belfast is spread out softly luminous below, and as the hill sweeps downwards, and the car gains its own eager momentum, I have the sensation of falling, in sudden relief, towards the city's gentle lights.

An interview with Lucy Caldwell

How have your personal experiences influenced the direction of your writing?

Everyone always assumes that my writing, especially *Where They Were Missed*, is strongly autobiographical. But it isn't at all! I had a very happy childhood, and my poor mother is horrified by the amount of people who've covertly wondered if she has an alcohol problem . . . In his essay *The Art of Fiction* Henry James writes of an English female novelist who was much praised for the 'accurate' depiction she'd given of French Protestant boys, and asked how long it had taken her to do the research. She replied that once, in Paris, she had been walking up a staircase when she had glimpsed some youths eating around a table with their minister. And from that moment, she had created the whole world of her novel. 'The glimpse made a picture', James writes, 'and it lasted only a moment, but that moment was experience.' I think that this explanation sums up perfectly what it is to write fiction: that although not everything I write about 'happened', all of it is in some sense 'true'.

As a writer, what would you say are the biggest challenges that you face?

As a writer of both novels and plays, my biggest challenge is always staying in control of whichever form I'm working in. If I've been writing a lot of prose, for example, I'll find myself giving characters in a play huge, eloquent, beautifully written speeches which are absolutely dead on stage – because, of course, in a play it isn't what a character is <u>saying</u> that matters, it's what they're <u>doing</u>, or in other words, <u>why</u> they're saying it. Similarly, if I've been spending a lot of time on a play, my prose tends to get a bit too dialogue-heavy.

What would you say sets the book apart from other things you have written?

I wrote it in my early twenties, before I'd ever read much Joyce, or Flaubert, or Dostoyevsky, or many of the other writers who are so important to me today. And because it is the first 'proper' thing I ever wrote, I think it has a rawness and energy and innocence that I'll never be able to capture again. But then again, in a funny sort of way every single thing that you write feels as if it's the first thing you've ever written . . .

In what way is it similar?

When I was growing up I couldn't wait to get away from Belfast. Once I left, I thought I'd never go back, and I was surprised – and not a little resentful – to find myself writing about Belfast. But I am increasingly conscious of writing in an Irish, and a Northern Irish, tradition – which, when you consider the great writers who have come from this part of the world, is something which makes me feel incredibly honoured and humble – and now I am ex-ceedingly proud to be Northern Irish. Although this is a horrible generalisation, I suppose that all of my writing, at some level, is 'about' Northern Ireland, or at least shares a concern about what it means to be Northern Irish.

Which writers have influenced you?

A couple of books that I think influenced *Where They Were Missed* are Seamus Deane's *Reading In The Dark* and Patrick McCabe's *The Butcher Boy*. Elizabeth Bowen and W. B. Yeats are two of my absolute favourite writers, and, in terms of playwrights, Chekhov, Maeterlinck and Brian Friel have been really important. But I think that most significant of all have been myths and folklore and fairytales – the idea of storytelling, and stories as a repository of cultural memory; the way we use stories to create and enforce and define who we are and where we come from. And of course many of the books I read as a child: Susan Cooper's *The Dark Is Rising* series, Laura Ingalls Wilder's *Little House On The Prairie* sequence, Richmal Crompton's *Just William . . .* books, also *Lorna Doone*, *Moonfleet*, all that sort of thing.